SHE WORE NOTHING UNDER THE MINK COAT.

She was naked . . . and young . . . and dead.

A MURDER BEGINS AND ENDS this story of scandal and tragedy in a college town. You'll meet some memorable characters here—most of them hair-raising —as novelist Vin Packer spins out a sinister excursion with the cool, campy kids of Far Point College, New York.

It's a wild, wild joyride—from Thunderbird to Bluebird, from classroom to Cheetah, with stops on the way at rent-by-the-hour motel rooms. You'll watch in horror as the Pucci-Plantagenet crowd burns up the roads, heading for that sickening, inevitable crash . . . that jolting confrontation with the reality they can't escape . . . with

THE HARE IN MARCH.

The Hare in March

Vin Packer

PROLOGUE BOOKS

F+W Media, Inc.

Published in electronic format by
PROLOGUE BOOKS
an imprint of F+W Media, Inc.
10151 Carver Road
Blue Ash, Ohio 45242
www.prologuebooks.com

eISBN 10: 1-4405-3703-8
eISBN 13: 978-1-4405-3703-5

POD ISBN 10: 1-4405-5609-1
POD ISBN 13: 978-1-4405-5609-8

This is a work of fiction. Names, characters, corporations, institutions,
organizations, events, or locales in this novel are either the product of the author's
imagination or, if real, used fictitiously. The resemblance of any character to actual
persons (living or dead) is entirely coincidental.

This work has been previously published in print format by:
The New American Library as a Signet Book.

<u>One</u>

At ten o'clock that warm March night, the Far Point, New York, prowl car turned into Grandview Park. Patrolman Burroughs yawned and tried to find a more comfortable position on the seat. He said, "Hey, Hopkins, it's a little early for a stroll down lovers' lane. There won't be anything doing here for another hour."

His partner said, "I feel generous tonight."

"I know what you mean. They're better off coming here to do a little necking than going into the city to booze it up."

"You're a square, you know that, Burroughs? The kids don't say 'necking' anymore. The expression is 'making out.'"

"Oh, yeah? I was sure it was 'spooning.'"

"My kid is always talking about making out. In my day, that meant going all the way. Only we didn't say we made out with a girl, we said we made a girl."

"*You*, Hopkins? *You* made girls? I bet you had to put bags over their heads first."

Hopkins chuckled. "What'd *you* do, Burroughs, date girls from the blind school? Did any of them get a look at you?"

They had been riding together for four years. Both of them were veterans, with over ten years in the department. They had a lot of other things in common too. In Far Point they lived within walking distance of one another; they were men in their middle forties, who had seen action in World War II. Burroughs had a nineteen-year-old son, and

5

Hopkins had two boys under ten, and one fourteen-year-old. Far Point was in Rockland County, on the Jersey side of the George Washington Bridge. Except for the war years, neither man had spent much time out of this part of the country.

It was against the law to stop in Grandview Park after seven at night. The local people knew that the winding road was a shortcut to Far Point from Route 9W, and there was no law forbidding traffic to pass through. Not more than twenty or thirty drivers a night used the shortcut; the others who turned into the park were usually headed for one of the little dead-end side roads, where picnickers stopped during the day. Most of them were students from Far Point College, a medium-sized, coeducational college located just outside the city, on a hill overlooking the Hudson River.

There were some Far Pointers who complained bitterly about these young strangers in their midst. They felt the college was too progressive: the students were allowed to have cars, and while there was a rule prohibiting intoxication, there was none prohibiting drinking. The local tavern owners were in sympathy with the complainers. There were not more than six bars near Far Point, all of them noisy with television and pinball machines, for Far Point was basically a factory town; none of the six would serve students. They argued that they did not want the responsibility—there were too many students with falsified credentials boosting their age; then too, kids could not hold their liquor. They were rowdy inside, and a menace on the road outside. . . . The truth was somewhere in between these facts, and the fact that the bars' best customers were workers from the Far Point Bag Company, and F.P.B.ers were notorious enemies of F.P.C.ers.

But the majority of Far Point's populace lived on the outskirts of the city. They were commuters to New York City. They were media people, lawyers, doctors, brokers—people of a sophisticated disposition. While they usually chose Ivy League schools for their own children, they enjoyed having F.P.C. in the community; they felt that the college added color to an otherwise dreary little area, whose prime feature was its proximity to Manhattan.

Burroughs and Hopkins were for the college, too. Burroughs' boy was a sophomore there; it looked as though Hopkins' oldest would not be admitted when he was college age, for his grades were only average, and the school demanded better of "townies." But there were two more at home; Hopkins would be delighted if even one of his boys made it.

Years of dealing with F.P.C.ers had shown them to be no different from any other group of young people, despite the fact most of them were brighter than local kids, and carried more pocket money. The majority were better drivers than most Far Pointers, and as for the drinking, the patrolmen had brought in many more factory workers on a 390, than collegians.

Still, there was reason for concern. The state of New Jersey's legal drinking age was twenty-one; New York's was eighteen. Most of the land on this side of the George Washington Bridge was in New Jersey. The narrow part that was New York, was cut up into little towns like Far Point, which were either hostile to the students or too seedy to attract them. Friday, Saturday, and Sunday nights they took off in their cars, bound for the other side of the bridge. Having made that much effort to be served alcohol, they often drank too much, and the liquor began catching up with them during their journeys back, along the Palisades Parkway. The situation was not crucial, but every month three or four students were stopped and warned, and sometimes charged.

This was the reason the police were not always meticulous about enforcing the law against after-dark parking in Grandview. The young people were safer going there. The police would make their patrol early in the evening, before the kids got there, or they would simply cruise very slowly by the parked cars, and flash their spotlight at the embracing couples. A few less stalwart ones would take the beam of light as a notice to evacuate, but most knew that it was merely a we've-got-our-eye-on-you warning, and they limited their action to the front seats, and refrained from tossing their beer cans out onto park property.

Burroughs looked out at the philodendron bushes which banked the road, and yawned again. "I don't envy these kids any. When I was their age, we had a *real* war, and a real excuse to speed up things in the romance department."

"I may never see you again, baby, and I love you so much, too."

Burroughs laughed. "Yeah." He sang, " 'Oh give me something to remember you by, when I am far away from you.' "

"How about 'You'd be *so nice* to come home to, you'd be

so nice by the fire; you'd be *so nice*, you'd be *par-a-dise*, to come home to and *love*.' That was Helen's and my song."

"And she married you after she heard you sing it? What'd you do, dope her?"

Hopkins sighed. "Those were the days!"

"The songs the kids sing today—I don't envy them."

"Me neither," Hopkins said. "My fourteen-year-old sits around singing this garbage about these footsteps running through an open meadow. What does it say? You know what the name of the band is, that the college hired for the Rabbit Hop tomorrow night? The Freaks. How do you like that?"

"What footsteps running through a meadow?"

"It's a song. It goes: 'If the sleep has left your ears you might hear footsteps running through an open meadow.'"

"You pulling my leg, Hopkins?"

"That's the way the song goes. Then it says not to be shook up if you hear these footsteps on the meadow, because it's only some guy chasing butterflies of love."

"And I suppose a bunch of long-haired pansies are singing it?"

"Listen, my kid's trying to grow his hair. I tell Helen if his hair gets—"

Burroughs interrupted. "What's that?"

Hopkins slowed up. "It looks like a car on the wrong side of the road. It's just sitting there."

"Yeah. Anybody inside?"

They pulled closer. Hopkins fixed his searchlight on the car.

"Someone's behind the wheel," said Burroughs.

"He's got someone with him, too."

Hopkins drew alongside the car. It was a 1957 Thunderbird. Hopkins recognized the year and the model right away. He was a car buff, and this was the classic Thunderbird, the two-seater with the round windows.

Neither man made a move to get out of the prowl car; there was seldom any occasion for it in the park. Usually it just took a word or two. Hopkins rolled down his window and called out, "Hey!"

The young man behind the wheel of the Thunderbird stared straight ahead, without acknowledging Hopkins' or Burroughs' presence. A girl with long blond hair spilling to her shoulders was leaning against the young man's chest.

Hopkins yelled again, "Hey!"

"Too much in love to say good night," said Burroughs. "I suppose I better get out."

"Check his license."

They rarely bothered with the procedure, but Hopkins had a funny feeling that the young man was stone drunk. He sat there like a stone, even when Burroughs went over and rapped on the window.

Burroughs said, "Come on, kid! Roll her down!"

Finally, the young man gazed up at Burroughs and very slowly unrolled his window.

"You asleep with your eyes open?" said Hopkins.

Burroughs said, "Let me see your license."

The boy didn't say anything. He wore a sports coat and a tie; he was a good-looking youngster, eighteen or nineteen, with a pleasant expression on his face. He was not smiling, but he did not have a sullen look either. He seemed quiet and cooperative, and not too surprised at the intrusion; certainly not frightened by it.

As he fumbled for his wallet, Burroughs said, "Do you know you're parked on the wrong side of the road?"

"Yes."

"How'd you get on the wrong side of the road?"

"I'm sorry."

"Have you been drinking?"

"I just had two drinks."

"You wouldn't kid me?"

"Just two."

"Then what the hell are you doing on the wrong side of the road?"

"The car stopped. I started it, and it stopped."

"Why didn't you go for help?"

"Where?"

"Go for help? Go into Far Point? Did you plan to sit here all night?"

"I don't know."

"Wake up your girl friend."

"She's very tired."

"Has she been drinking too?"

"Neither of us had more than two. I'm sure of that."

"Why are you having such trouble talking then?"

"I'm not."

"It takes you a long time to say anything. Why is that?"

"I don't know for sure. But I can't find my wallet."

"Have you been driving without a license?"

"She was driving. Then I tried, and the car stopped."

Burroughs turned to Hopkins. "No license."

"I heard."

Hopkins had the same reluctance Burroughs had about making an arrest. . . . Still, no license, the wrong side of the road. . . . Hopkins said, "Tell him to get out of the car and walk in front of my headlights. See if he walks straight."

"Do it," Burroughs ordered the young man.

Gently, the boy eased the girl back so that her head rested against the seat, and her body leaned into it. She did not wake up. She was wearing a mink coat, a double-breasted sports style, with a belt in back. There was a blue chiffon scarf tied around her neck.

"Won't the car start?" Burroughs asked the boy, as the boy got out.

"Well, it did. Then it stopped."

"Walk!" Burroughs ordered.

The boy seemed to move in slow motion.

Hopkins said, "Ask him what his name is, if he goes to F.P.C."

Instead, Burroughs said, "Okay, son, let's go to the station."

Burroughs turned to Hopkins. "He's got a lump on his head, and he's barefoot."

"What?"

"He's barefoot. He's got a lump on his head the size of an egg."

Burroughs turned back to the boy, who stood there in the shine of the spotlight, holding his sports coat to his neck. "Come on, son. You've got yourself a snootful, haven't you? Did you fall?"

"I don't know why I took my shoes off. I'm not drunk."

"You're not some nut from Rockland State, are you?"

"No."

"Okay. You're not loose from the funny farm, so you have to be drunk, don't you? Or do you always go around like this?"

"It's just tonight."

"I see. Well, I wouldn't take you in any other night, son. Just tonight. Now c'mon. I have a car waiting for us."

"Her car goes," said the boy, walking very slowly toward Burroughs.

"We'll take my car," Burroughs said. "See? I got me a nice chauffeur named Hopkins, so leave the driving to us."

"All right."

"Do your feet hurt? Something wrong with your feet?"

"No."

"Then move, buddy. The pavement's nice and smooth."

The boy inched toward the prowl car.

Hopkins got out and went across to him. He said, "Are you glued together, or what?" He took the boy's arm, to help him.

The boy smiled. "I feel as though I'm coming unglued."

"Where've you been, boy?"

"At the house. I think I was, earlier."

"The house? Do you mean a fraternity house?"

"Yes."

Burroughs opened the door of the Thunderbird. He called in, "Wake up, little Suzy."

"She won't," the boy said. "She's too exhausted."

Hopkins said, "What fraternity do you belong to, kid?"

"Pi Delta Pi."

"A Pi Pi, huh?"

"Yes."

"Burroughs? Did you hear this? He's a Pi Pi."

Burroughs was saying, "Come on now. Rise and shine, little lady."

Hopkins said, "Do you know Bud Burroughs?"

"Yes. Bud."

"That's his old man."

Then Burroughs called out, "Hopkins?"

"What?"

"Put the cuffs on him."

"He's okay."

"Put them on!"

Hopkins had often heard an angry tone in Burroughs' voice, but never one with this edge of panic added.

Quickly, Hopkins reached to his side for the handcuffs. The boy waited, holding up his wrists to make it easier for Hopkins.

Then Hopkins walked over to the Thunderbird, pulling the boy with him, as though he were drag weight.

Burroughs' voice cracked. "I'm pretty sure she's dead."

She was also naked under the fur coat, slumped back against the right car door, with blood running from her breasts down the white skin of her body.

"Oh, Jesus Christ!" Hopkins said. *"Oh, God!"*

He turned his head away, found himself staring into the boy's face.

"She couldn't help it," the boy whispered.

There were tears flooding his eyes.

Two

Charles Shepley's roommate was always fooling with a tape recorder. Two days before the murder in Grandview Park, his latest results were playing in their room at the Pi Pi house, an anastomosis of Staff Sergeant Barry Sadler's "The Ballad of the Green Berets" with the Beatles' "Nowhere Man."

STAFF. SGT. SADLER (*drum rolls in the background*): "Fighting soldiers from the sky."
THE BEATLES (*guitars twanging*): "Real nowhere man."
STAFF SGT. SADLER: "Fearless men who jump and die."
THE BEATLES: "In a nowhere land."
STAFF SGT. SADLER: "Men who mean just what they say."
THE BEATLES: "For nobody."

"Like it, Shep?"
"It's all right."
The room smelled of rubbing alcohol and Pub. Dan Thorpe wanted to be a writer (he was midway through a very staccato book; all the conversation was preceded by dashes instead of quotation marks). Ever since he had read in Hotchner's book that Papa preferred sponge baths with rubbing alcohol, he had not been near soap and water, which was why he needed help from Revlon, and doused himself with their male fragrance.
"Why just all right?"

"Not *just* all right; it's all right. It's okay."

"You like it?"

Charles said he did; why start with Dan?

They had been roommates since they pledged Pi Pi in October. By this time, Charles was resigned to most of the facts involving Daniel Quentin Thorpe III.

That Thorpe loved his body, even his eyelids, which were now being soothed by two damp Oculine eye pads, as he stretched out in his red-and-white-polka-dot shorts, atop his Bates bedspread, a copy of *Ramparts*, open to an article berating the C.I.A., containing his Mexsana-powdered feet.

That Thorpe read I.F. Stone religiously, learning the weekly newsletter like a catechism; that you never really had an argument with Dan, but with I.F., or Murray Kempton, or James A. Wechsler, or Far Point College's lone way-out leftist Dr. Dowdy, who taught Dialectical Materialism and considered himself a Maoist.

That Thorpe, a nice enough guy, well-meaning and wholesome, was too much hot air, always overdid everything, worked too painstakingly at something which was not that important, usually went over the way this thing playing did, this crossing of the Beatles and the staff sergeant; the *time* involved, just to get:

STAFF SGT. SADLER: "Back at home, a young wife waits."
(*ta dot, dot, da!*)
THE BEATLES: "You don't know what you're missing."
(*twang!*)
STAFF SGT. SADLER: "Her Green Beret has met his fate."
(*ta, dot, dot, da!*)
THE BEATLES: "He's a real nowhere man." (*twang!*)

"Shep?"

"Hmmm?"

"What are you doing?"

"What am I doing? Listening to your creation, Dan. I mean, I'm not coming because of it, or anything."

"You're not sitting up and could toss a robe over me?"

"Negative."

"Okay. I freeze to death."

"It's like the end of spring out."

"I hope it lasts through Friday. Who you dragging to the Rabbit Hop?"

"Lois."

"Did Blouter give you his permission?"

"That rule doesn't apply to the school dances, just the ones we give here at the house. I don't need his permission."

"I forgot. The school doesn't object, just the fraternity. It takes a heap of anti-Semitism to make a home a house."

"Thorpe, she doesn't give a damn and I don't either."

"I'd like to figure out what you *do* give a damn about."

"Work at it, then . . . If you care so damn much, why don't *you* depledge?"

"Termites work better from the inside than the outside."

"Oh, I see. You're going to change things."

"I'm going to try, Shep. I hope that in four years when I leave this place, no Pi Pi pledge will have to *ask* if he can date a Jewish girl."

"Yawn."

"Or even a Negro girl."

"Snore."

"Very blasé cat, aren't you, Shepley? What *does* get you excited?"

"Sex."

It was at this point in the conversation that Pi Pi Pledge Director Peter Hagerman charged into the room.

"What are your names, farts?" he barked.

Thorpe jumped to his feet. "I'm Daniel Quentin Thorpe the Third, sir."

Charles stood up too. "Charles Shepley, sir."

"Charles Shepley what, creep?"

There was no love between Hagerman and Shepley, but Shepley knew some things about Hagerman instinctively, as an animal will sometimes be oversensitive to the quirks of another animal, a hostile animal. Shepley knew that while it was common practice to address the pledges as "Fart" Hagerman hated saying the word. Hagerman could make almost any other scene, but not that word; that word made him choke.

"Charles Shepley is my name, sir."

"Your name is Creep."

"Yes, sir."

"What's your name, Creep?"

"My name is Creep, sir."

"You're a liar, pledge. Your name is Fuckface."

"Yes, sir. My name is Fuckface." Good. Hagerman could handle that, and it had a nice, virile sound to it. Hagerman looked relieved. To Shepley, the word was comical; he wondered if he could control an impulse to grin. Hagerman told

him not to, with one black look. What was it between Hagerman and him? Hagerman had seemed to dislike him instantly.
That had been very clear during the second night of Rush,
when Blouter had taken Shepley aside and said, "Charles,
officially we're not supposed to ask yet, but how about it?
Are you with the Pi Pi's?"

"Yes, thanks." Handshake; he was pocket-pledged.

"Fine, Charles!" and Blouter had pounded Charles's back
and called over Peter Hagerman.

Hagerman was very short; he had that certain tortured
Mickey Rooney expression a lot of little men possessed, who
seemed comfortable only when they sat down, and posed for
photographs on stairways standing one step above a woman
to be taller than she was, and as boys had stuffed paper in
their shoes to seem taller; and Hagerman was a clotheshorse,
like so many of them; he was one of the few Pi Pi's who
had real diamonds in his diamond-shaped Pi Pi pin.

And that night he had not said, "Oh, good!" or "Glad to
hear it!" or anything superfluous, but simply, "Where you
from, Shepley?"

"New York."

"City?"

"Yes."

Blouter, hungry always for yaks and fun, had interrupted.
"He has a gas of an act, Pete. Charles, do the imitations."

Which always made it awful, a command performance,
bark like a seal, be funny like a new pledge all the brothers
are crazy about, and Charles prefaced what he said with a
shrug he had not planned on, and heard his own voice make
very dull something which was often very funny. "I collect
rumors. I imitate someone, and you have to guess the rumor."

"Let's hear," said Hagerman, poker-faced, cracking his
knuckles impatiently, as though he wondered how Blouter
could ever have gotten him into this.

"Well, here's one: You're loaded now, doll; get some sleep
and then call me at Peter's. Don't forget now; be sure to call
no matter what."

Charles had screwed up the line and his Boston accent had
come out poorly. Blouter said, "You changed it," disappointed.

"I'm not with it, I guess."

"Who is it?" Hagerman asked.

Blouter said, "What famous contemporary martyr was supposed to be with what famous contemporary suicide, on the night of her demise?"

"Bull!" said Hagerman. "I heard it was Bobby, anyway."

And he had walked away, and Charles had thought to himself that he would get even with him for it one day, which was a very unCharlesy thought circa Rush Week.

"Fuckface," said Hagerman, "I think I'll give you the news first, because you're the one pledge who's going to see a er-really big shew, so hear this, Pledge Fuckface: 'Lasciate ogni speranza, voi ch'entrate!' "

Beside Charles, Dan Thorpe moaned.

What Hagerman was saying was that The Divine Comedy had begun. During World War II, Hell Week had been abolished by the F.P.C. fraternities as adolescent behavior. For about twenty years the frats had been Goody-Two-shoes', hustling their pledges down to Far Point's Negro district with food packages and tool kits with which to make house repairs, instead of beating their balls red, and leaving them barefoot in their jockey shorts on back roads a hundred miles from the house. Then in the sixties the Greeks had held a series of solemn conclaves given over to philosophizing about why frat life no longer had any real p'zazz, and was not what was happening anymore at all on a campus, and a Deke said frat life had started turning off when the traditions were taken away one by one. Bring them back. Bring back Hell Week; call it angel food cake, if necessary, but order up those wooden paddles and fix up those old blood-letting rituals, and the tears would be back again in the eyes of the men receiving their pins in the initiation ceremony. This would make for bigger and better alumni donations in the future; Keep Greek Town Green.

A Beta said the only safe way to get away with it, since the President of F.P.C. was not a frat fan, was to cut Hell Week down to a few days, give it another name, and have it at separate times.

Pi Delta Pi chose to have it at a different time each year in order to keep the pledges in suspense; they organized it into a three-day period. The Divine Comedy began with the Day of Inferno, during which the boys were hazed in whatever way the Pledge Director devised. The Day of Purgatorio followed—the pledges were assigned various duties, some benefiting the community, some the house, some a Pi Pi date's car or the rec room of her sorority house, or the front sidewalk of a female dormitory. On the last day, Day of

Paradiso, Pi Pi pledges became members. Membership usually carried with it a special surprise for each pledge, a particular thing he wanted. Last year, Bud Burroughs had been presented with a life-size, cut-out photograph, mounted on cardboard, of Ursula Andress. Made from a film clip of *The Tenth Victim*, it showed her in a silver bikini, with a blazing bra revealing two guns blasting bullets at the pull of an underarm trigger.

At the announcement, in Italian, "Abandon hope, all ye that enter," the pledge was notified that The Divine Comedy would commence in exactly twenty hours; he was to answer, in Italian, "Conosco i segni dell' antica fiamma." (I recognize the signals of the ancient flame.) The Pledge Director would then present him with his individual itinerary.

But Charles Shepley stood dumbstruck; despite all the drills in pledge class, he could not remember a word of the Italian response.

In the background,

STAFF SGT. SADLER: "Put silver wings on my son's chest."
THE BEATLES: "He's as blind as he can be."
STAFF SGT. SADLER: "Make him one of America's best."
THE BEATLES: "He's a real nowhere man."
STAFF SGT. SADLER: "He'll be a man, they'll test one day."
THE BEATLES: "You don't know what you're missing."
STAFF SGT. SADLER: "Have him win the Green Beret."
THE BEATLES: "For nobody."

Finally, Shepley said, "Sir? I forgot the Italian."
"You *what*?"
"I forgot the Italian, sir."
Hagerman's face got very red; he began clearing his throat, a sure sign he was trying to bring himself under control so his words would not come out garbled. He could go to pieces all of a sudden. The pledges had seen this side of Hagerman often. Charles Shepley had seen it more often than most, but Dan had been its catalyst too. Hagerman, for example, had done a long, laudatory term paper for American Civilization on Peter Dawkins; and Hagerman's grim countenance that afternoon had not been softened any by the blasphemous rendition from the Webcor atop Thorpe's bureau.

"Thorpe?" said Hagerman. *"Thorpe?"*
"Ye-yes, sir."

" 'Lasciate ogni speranza, voi ch'entrate!' "

"Ah. Um. Cocono . . . Ah, I know this, sir, like the back of my hand, if I may just go slowly."

"You may not, you goddam fuckface Vietnik! Spit it out!"

"Cocono . . . cocono . . . I—I'm blocked."

"Spit it out!"

"I can't, I tell you!"

"Spit it out, you prick! You get those wop words out of you, you mother!"

"Coco . . . co . . . co . . ."

Thorpe stopped like a train unchugging and coming to a halt; he stood there, his tall skinny body shivering—he was always cold, even in the middle of summer, and goose bumps began on his arms. He rubbed them, studying them tenderly, as though the poor things were awfully sick and needed him; his pinched-in little waist barely assumed the responsibility of holding up the silk polka dot shorts. Every now and then Dan jerked them up above the waist; it took some seconds for them to start the very slow descent.

Hagerman took two manila envelopes from the inside pocket of his tweed jacket with its leather elbow patches. He looked around the room until he spotted a wastebasket.

"Empty that basket on your bed, pledge."

Charles sighed; it was a bad day for this. He had emptied his electric pencil sharpener in there; he had ripped up into hundreds of little pieces his weekly allotment of three letters from his mother, who was thirty-five minutes, or fifty cents, away from him, yet still wrote, sometimes six pages back and front, and he had emptied the ash trays that had collected for days in the room. Old tube of Crest. Empty packs of Marlboros. (Dan, who didn't smoke, always said, "Come to Marlboro Country where the big C is boss!"). Empty package of Lorna Doones. Empty box of Ritz crackers, not empty of crumbs. Dirty Q-tips from a vigorous ear-cleaning session. *Yyikh!*

He did it, bravely—he had changed the sheets that morning.

"Set the wastebasket in the center of the floor, Shepley."

Charles had a feeling Hagerman was going to command him to urinate into the basket, something like that. He didn't feel *at all* like any of that crap today. The latest letter from his mother, which he had not yet ripped into shreds, the seven-pager which he had found in his box at the house that noon when he came home for Pi Pi chili-chow had depressed the hell out of him. He had not admitted that to himself before this moment when he stood there with the wastebasket between Hagerman and himself. He could feel its bulge in the back pocket of his corduroys.

I hope you will not forget Paris, France, and the custom you learned there of pouring a little of the newly opened wine into your own glass first, to accept cork remnants which are often unavoidable, for these are the things which do impress so very much the daughters of the better class, and Charles, *you know me* well enough to appreciate that I do not necessarily mean $$$, for it cannot buy happiness. Though we were a happy family when we had it, for life is easier, and now we eat humble pie.

Into the wastebasket, Peter Hagerman tossed the manila envelopes.

He said, "Thorpe, you fuckface, put a match to them."

Thorpe took out a silver lighter and rolled it to a flame, while Hagerman's vein on the left of his forehead throbbed against the skin and his eyes bulged and he began to scream, "Is that a match, mother? Is that a mother-loving, screwing-mother match, or is that a lighter belonging to a frigging fuckface of a fruity prick?"

Still, he couldn't handle fart. He'd probably been traumatized as a child, same as Charles. Charles's trauma was what both his mother and father called a bowel movement. It was called a "boom-boom." He used to blush in the middle of war games, having to run fast behind a bush, grabbing leaves to take with him; he had been like one of Pavlov's dogs; all he needed to hear was *Boom! Boom!* and he fell open.

Dan had located a match; he bent over the wastebasket like someone afflicted with Parkinson's, scratching and scratching, then finally finding a flame to touch to the envelopes.

"Those," said Hagerman with beady eyes, "*were* your itineraries. Those were rather typical itineraries, even though my reaction to you is not a typical reaction, for I dare venture no pledge director in the history of Pi Delta Pi fraternity, in the history of any fraternity, has ever *loathed* two pledges so very, very deeply. I deeply loathe you. You are not fit to accompany the other pledges on the Inferno; therefore, I have burned your itineraries."

For some reason, in a slow few seconds of silence that followed, Dan Thorpe croaked, "Thank you."

For what? Weren't they depledged now?

    . . . though I am not one to make a thing of fraternities, your father is very pleased, so pleased, really, Charles, at your being a second-generation Pi Delta Pi, and I have heard him make mention of a mother's pin, which the mother of a member may wear, and though I am not much for cheap costume jewelry, having been used to the real thing, it would so please your father that I wonder if . . .

"Why did I burn these itineraries, Shepley? I loathe *you* so that you should feel my very thoughts frying your skin, baking their way into your yellow guts!"

"I suppose we're depledged."

"No such mother-loving luck, Shepley! You are on room quarantine, Shepley! You are on room quarantine, Thorpe! You are to stay in your rooms from now until the time I have sat down and put my mind to composing the most vile and fittingly degrading itineraries I have ever created. You are not to eat or take a leak or use the phone; you are in room quarantine and you are to keep it until I come back with Infernos."

After he had banged out of the room, Shepley said, "Turn that music off! That got us into all this!" knowing full well that was not true.

"If *you'd* remembered, *I* wouldn't have gotten rattled."

"I'm not taking the blame for it."

"Don't blame my tape then."

STAFF SGT. SADLER: "Trained to live off nature's land."
THE BEATLES: "Nowhere land."
STAFF SGT. SADLER: "Trained in combat hand to heepity, heepity, heepity, yart—"

Thorpe pressed the *Off* button finally; he was still shaking. When he was this way—not often; usually Hagerman was the cause—then Charles felt something for him. For one thing, Dan looked so vulnerable half-naked, skin and bones, like some old emaciated philosopher from India in diapers and on a three-peas-a-day diet until single-handed he brought about CHANGE; for another reason, poor Dan, out to save

the Vietnamese from the Green Berets, and the Mississippi
Negroes from the Mississippi whites, and the Lois Fayes from
the Pi Delta Pis—and a five-foot runt son of a Mad Avenue
ad man leaves his bones loose and rattling.

Charles said, "Hagerman's bark is worse than Hagerman's
bite."

"I don't know, Shep."

"And there are rules, Dan. He has to stay within bounds
or the whole Panhellenic Society will have his head."

"But that temper of his, Shep. Like, Pow! Zap! It gets
way out of proportion with what's happened, doesn't it?"

" 'Conosco i segni dell' antica fiamma,' " Charles Shepley
said. "*Now* I remember."

"Dear God," said Dan Thorpe, standing in the center of
the room, his eyes closed, his hands palms-up, pressed together in prayer, "get Hagerman for us, Lord. Let him break
his neck going downstairs, Holy Father. Smash him up some
way, our Lord in Heaven to whom we dedicate our lives; I
mean, really give Hagerman the business, Sir!"

Shepley walked over to his bed, carrying the charred tin
wastebasket and the cardboards from two shirt backs; he
began to scrape up the cracker crumbs and pencil shavings
and pieces of his mother's letter.

"God is dead, Thorpe," said Shepley.

Three

Shepley took advantage of the quarantine to reread his mother's letter, while Dan went to the typewriter to work on Chapter Ten of his novel, which was about a Green Beret AWOL, anti-Hemingway in its philosophy, but Papa all the way in style. It began:

Jack didn't like war very much. He didn't like to know there was nothing much left of the rich flat lands south of the Vaico Oriental River. He didn't like kill ratio. He didn't like napalm. He didn't like Dean Rusk. He didn't like Robert McNamara.

Natalie Shepley's letter began:

Dearest Charles first read the piece about your brother which I have copied from New York East a small neighborhood but very good newspaper word for word. I would have sent the clipping but I wanted one for Aunt Martha and another for Aunt Agnes which left me only one for myself as I had just three copies of the paper. But I have not left a word out.

Then, in another color ink—green—with no paragraph to separate it from the body of the letter, carefully printed, with capital letters for the headline:

MOTHER'S THERE BUT HE CAN'T SEE HER BRAVE SMILE. New York, N.Y. March 20 (AP) Billy Shepley's eyes were open, but he could not see his mother's brave smile. His face was turned toward his mother, but he could not hear her cheerful chatter. He probably will never hear her voice again, never see her adoring face again, never even register the fact that she is there, every day, to visit him. Six years ago Billy had an accident in the family car, and since then he has not been conscious. His mother sits by his bedside reading to him. The nuns of Holy Child give him his meals through a feeding tube every three hours. The doctors stop in once a day. But Billy is unaware of all of it; he will live on never knowing he is loved and cared for, because the damage to his nervous system is permanent. Billy has a strong heart, and he is only 23; he may live a very long time. But people, some people in this age of cynicism, still believe in miracles, and Natalie Shepley is one of these people. She is gay and busy during her visits with her son. "I could let this get me down," she said, "but I don't. I believe that one day Billy's going to be A-Okay, and I don't mind sounding foolish, if that's how I sound. I have a lot of faith in Billy; that's how I manage to keep my chin up.

Change to Waterman's blue:

I thought it was so nice of the newspaper to print this piece about Billy, and it is enough of an Easter gift for me. If you want a copy you can write to the newspaper for one, Charles. Address: 231 East 86 Street, New York, New York 10028. On Easter Sunday I am taking him a calla lily begonia, which has a nice flowery smell and Aunt Agnes is sending him a cyclamen which does not smell but has beautiful blossoms. Cut flowers die so quickly and the nuns have enough to do without changing their water, so I tell people to send him plants instead. His room is so cheery as you know with the blue walls and I have out some of his things like the green and white Michigan State banner where he so dearly wanted to go plus the photograph of Janie who as you know is married now to someone else but would not mind I'm sure. (She still sends X-mas card to him each year at Christmas, did you know that?) He has good color in his face and is a brick about what has befallen him, and his eyes tell me not to worry and I try not to. Send him a humorous Easter card, Charles, not the sick sort but a nice Hallmark as it would mean so much to him. I read cards he receives aloud to him. He always had such a good sense of humor, don't you think? So much for Billy, though I do not mean that the way it sounds, for I do not begrudge him one cent of all the money he has cost us, for what kind of a life does he have after all, and we are able to walk and laugh and pray for him.

How are you, dear? It has been several weeks since we have heard and I do not like to call you at Pi Pi like a mother hen, but I do wonder if you are coming home for Easter dinner and a visit to Billy, and to stay for a few days. Charles, though I am not one to make a thing of fraternities, your father is very pleased, so pleased, really, Charles, at your being a second-generation Pi Delta Pi, and I have heard him make mention of a mother's pin, which the mother of a member may wear, and though I am not much for cheap costume jewelry, having been used to the real thing, it would so please your father that I wonder if you were considering getting me some small Easter remembrance you would want to make it a pin with the Pi Pi crest. Do not go to any trouble for me but if you feel like it I would be happy to please your father in this small way. He is busy with his bugs and I sometimes think Billy will forget who he is if he does not visit him more often, but his job at the institute is so demanding, and for such a small return too. I hope you will think of this when you choose your field, for science unless it is moon-launching and bombs is not rewarding look at your father. If we did not have the income from the money Grandpa Shepley left us we would not be able to keep Billy at Holy Child and you would not even be at Far Point College which was not my dream for you anyway. It is all right to be a Pi Pi but when you are out in the world people's ears would pick up more if you could say I was a Princeton man. They do not have fraternities but being a Pi Pi never did a thing for your father after he left Michigan State that I know of. So Charles think carefully about your future for if you cannot get somewhere saying you were a Princeton man or a Yale man, then you must have a field that pays. I would not have married your father on his salary but you see we always thought we would have Grandpa Shepley's money for extras, not knowing what Fate had in store for Billy.

Are you dating nice girls, Charles? I hope you will not forget Paris, France, and the custom you learned there of pouring a little of the newly opened wine into your own glass first, to accept cork remnants which are often unavoidable, for these are the things which do impress so very much the daughters of the better class, and Charles *you know me* well enough to appreciate that I do not necessarily mean $$$, for it cannot buy happiness. Though we were a happy family when we had it, for life is easier, and now we eat humble pie. I will say one thing for your father his sophisticated ways impressed me the way he knew little things like the tipping of the wine steward in a good restaurant and the English names for French dishes and these are the things you should bear in mind for girls of good families look for these little things believe me. What are some of the things the fathers of the girls you are dating do? These things interest me though you do not seem to pick up on it. A fraternity should broaden you and there is no reason to think you would not have been a Pi Pi if your father had not been one at M.S.U. for I hear they often do not take a legacy, so you got there because you are real Pi Pi material, and never forget that Charles, and live up to it, for you are all we can truly count on if something does not happen soon where Billy is concerned.

All right Charles I won't take up any more of your time since I know you are busy but we are having ham for dinner on Easter, and going to Holy Child about three that afternoon and Billy will know if you are not present this I can promise. Think of what his life is like and do not begrudge him that little joy he has so little. If you remember to do something about the mother's pin okay but if you don't I will understand. Study hard and consider a good job in the future. Love from your mother Natalie Shepley.

In black ink at the bottom of the last page, Clinton Shepley had written a few lines:

C.

Trust mother wrote all the news. Working with praying mantes this week. You know they usually (females) decapitate their lovers, which solves the mantis population explosion, but one we have is indefatigable. Still a virgin, but has beheaded seventeen partners in one week. We call her Lolita (ha! ha!). Billy doesn't know the difference between a bunch of tulips and a half-dozen popsicle sticks, though I cannot get N.S. to accept this, so if she is trying to talk you into sending him an Easter plant, save your allowance for other things. Send him a card to please her, though. Better still, make the journey across the miles and let us feast our eyes on you, but only if you feel like it. Not as a duty. Affectionately, Father.

There was never any reference to Pi Delta Pi in the messages Charles's father scribbled at the bottom of Natalie Shepley's letters. Charles's mother had done a neat pre-enrollment job of brainwashing Charles into believing he should suffer the agonies of Rush Week for his father's sake. Ingenuous as she often seemed, she was not without guile, for the only person she asked to do anything for *her* sake was Billy. ("Billy, it's Mother; aren't you going to smile for me? I came all the way here in the pouring rain for your smile, Billy.")

Rush Week was no picnic. Charles was not fraternity material, and all the frats but Pi Pi picked up on it immediately. He had received exactly two return bids after the initial day of rushing—one for the third day (pig day, in the middle of the week) at Rho Kappa, a fraternity that was not national and always had a huge quota to fill, and the prize second-day bid from Pi Pi. It was true that Pi Pi did not always pledge legacies, so Charles was amazed when Blouter pocket-pledged him on Number Two night of Rush Week. There was nothing wrong with the way Charles looked; he was no different from a score of other average-looking young men in button-down shirts and Ivy, hopsack, Glen, J. Press, Fortrel polyester, and Zantrel 700 rayon suits; sandy-haired, five foot eleven, blue-eyed, no pimples, no speech impediment, good teeth—it was his attitude which was wrong. The back slapping, the lusty-voiced singing of "Banging Away on Lulu," the beer-guzzling false euphoria, the asinine speeches

("Men! Welcome aboard *S.S.* Pi Pi! We keep a tight ship, men! We're tight every goddam night, men! We like our women tight, men! We like a wet deck!"—pause for laughter and applause, then solemnly—"To be serial a second, men. Pi Delta Pi was founded in 1891. We represent the very best in ——"); it was the whole schmear. Charles's face was worn out from forcing his mouth to smile; his face had actually ached at the end of Number One day. The Greeks could spot a lead foot; back at the dorm where the rushees were housed during their ordeal. Dan Thorpe had commented on Charles's meager return of two envelopes:

"Even Dillon got six returns, and he has pimples the size of pool balls. What'd you do?"

"I don't know, but I must be doing something wrong."

"Well, forget about it. Go for Pi Pi. They hear your music, and they're first rate. I'm going Pi Pi if I can."

"I don't know how I got a Two. I nearly fell asleep there."

"Stay awake and don't ask . . . You're not a legacy, are you?"

"Yes, but they don't take legacies unless they want them."

"Oh," Thorpe had said. That answered it for Thorpe.

But after Charles had been pledged, he found out two other Pi Pi legacies had not received bids. He felt better, but he still could not explain it. Except maybe it was Mike Blouter. He was the only one Charles had hit it off with, and Mike was Pi Pi's president. Charles never could turn on just for anyone, but he could for Mike; he had made Mike laugh without even trying; talking with Mike, he was not aware he was keeping up a conversation, as he was so painfully aware of doing at other houses, with other Greeks. Except for Mike, Charles could not make the scene at Rush Week; he went over like he did with Peter Hagerman, over and out.

Blouter seemed to take the whole Greek bit with a grain of salt; he was Greek Town's Dean Martin, always a little unsteady on his pins, enjoying his reputation as a booze hound, but sharp, admired—the type who could call the whole frat system an adolescent bag, and get away with it.

If Charles had had to go to anyone but Blouter for permission to ask Lois Faye to the house, he might have brought the minuscule left of his mother's world crashing to her feet by turning in his pledge pin.

With Blouter it was not as hard:

"What's her last name?"

"Faye."

"Is she an A E Pi or a Zeta?"

"She's not in a Jewish sorority. She's only half-Jewish."

"They'd take her anyway, does she know that?"

"She doesn't want to be in a sorority."

"What's she want with a goy like you?"

"She likes the way I dance. You know, the Jews have a natural sense of rhythm."

"I heard that. They're smart about music like the Negroes are about money."

"It's okay then?"

"Do you have to ask?"

"Would I ask if I didn't have to?"

"She won't have to teach you anything about *chutzpah*, Shepley."

So a Blouter, for Charles, made up for a Hagerman; good food and a Sears-O-Pedic Innerspring Sleep Set took the edge off candlelit song fests in the Pi Pi Pub, a replica of an English tavern located next to the furnace room; the thought of a mother pin fastened to Natalie Shepley's sparse bosom made up for The Divine Comedy (Charles hoped).

Keep on keeping on, Charles's father was fond of saying, a winner never quits and a quitter never wins . . . at least he *had* been fond of saying that, before William Shepley downed a dozen rum-and-Cokes one Saturday evening some six years ago, got into the family Buick, and missed his chance to belong to the Pepsi generation. Billy even missed his chance to belong to the ages. ("I bet you can hear me, Billy. Mother bets that.")

Charles grabbed a sheet of Pi Pi stationery from his desk drawer and snapped the end of his pen to put the ball point ready for action. His mother liked him to write his letters on the official fraternity paper, ". . . *not that I care, but your father reads your letters too, and I like to pass them at my Tuesday brunches. I'd be glad to send you money to pay for it if it's the expense that makes you write on ordinary notebook paper and sometimes actual scrap paper.*"

Charles wrote:

Dear Folks,

Glad to see Billy made the news. Too bad he can't be on television as well. Yes, I remember Billy's sense

of humor. Beautiful! I die laughing every time I think
of the day Billy put the Annerman's Siamese in their
Coldspot Upright Freezer while they were at the
movies. What a comedian! Did that cat ever look
funny stiff as a board and dead as a doornail!

List of the things the fathers of the girls I'm dating do:
1. Hustle for the buck. (Not that it can buy happiness.)
2. Get juiced at the local country club on week-
ends.
3. Burn crosses at Klan gatherings.
4. Watch Gomer Pyle on television.
5. Support Ronald Reagan.
6. Attend Yale reunions.
7. Pour a little of the newly opened wine into
their own glasses first, to accept cork remnants.
8.

Then Charles wadded up the stationery and tossed it into
the wastebasket.

Dan Thorpe said, "I wonder what Hagerman is dreaming
up for us right now."

"Maybe it'll be a welcome relief." said Charles.

"Now what the hell does *that* mean?"

"I don't know."

"I don't know what the hell that means either."

But Charles Shepley knew. He meant what it was like that
summer when what had happened to Billy really began to hit
home, after the doctors stopped skirting around the plain
fact that Billy was and would always be a vegetable, and
there was no Princeton in Charles's future anymore, no more
point to cracking the books the way he did, nor to dreaming
the dreams he did, the corny all-American shiny-faced own
his-own-sports-car fantasies, wear a cap and run down to
P.J.'s with a girl and be like Billy bigshot bubbles . . . that
summer would have been impossible had Charles not had all
the trouble with his teeth, because the deeper the dentist
drilled into his nerves, the more he scraped at the rawness of
his gums, the greater the physical pain, the less the gnawing
hatred of Billy, the really murderous hatred of Billy, always just below the surface, then spilling over the top, leav-

ing him awake nights to confront ghostly Billys in the dark of his bedroom, with a switchblade sprung and ready in his hand; in the dentist's chair it was a welcome relief.

One letter like that from his mother could do it, start it up again, even make Hagerman's idea of hell seem less like hell.

Four

When Bud Burroughs came back from lab that afternoon, he was busting to tell someone about it, but Hagerman was his only confidant in Pi Pi, and Hagerman was in a bad mood.

"I am goddam sick and tired of that mother-loving thing on the wall," said Hagerman, after Burroughs had tossed his books on the bed, and begun to change his pants; "goddam fed up seeing it day after day."

"Jesus, Peter, it was your idea in the first place."

"Jesus Peter is tired of it, Burroughs!"

"Then take it down."

Hagerman was talking about the life-size Ursula Andress poster over Burroughs' desk. Hagerman was sitting on the floor in a silk blue-and-white Pi Pi robe, cross-legged with his clipboard propped against his knees, staring up at it.

"You take it down, Burroughs!"

Burroughs stepped out of his pants and crossed the room in his stocking feet and gave a yank forceful enough to jolt his spectacles to the end of his nose and bring the poster crashing to the floor.

"Okay now? Okay now, Peter?"

"Well, what the hell is eating _you_, Burroughs?"

"Wasn't that an order? It sounded like an order."

"Goddam it, I've got enough trouble without your prima donna scenes!"

"Jesus, Peter, I come home pretty excited about something that happened today, and I'm not in the room ten seconds before you start chewing me out! I didn't even have my pants off before you started in on me!"

"What got you so excited, Burroughs? Did your old man let you play with his gun?"

"Get off my back about my old man. You don't like your old man—okay—but I like mine."

"I know you do, Burroughs. You're a cop-lover."

"Knock it off, Peter! I mean it."

"You ought to live at home, Burroughs. You could play with your old man's gun every night . . . Hey, *that's* a thought!"

"Every time you're in a lousy mood, you start on my old man!"

"Wait a minute! That's a thought!"

Burroughs didn't care to hear the thought. He was sore at Hagerman now. He went across to the closet and pulled a pair of old khakis from a hook. Peter was right about one thing: Burroughs *ought* to live at home. It was costing Burroughs' father a hundred dollars extra a month for Burroughs to live at Pi Pi, and that spelled s-a-c-r-i-f-i-c-e on a policeman's salary. Burroughs' father was making this sacrifice so Burroughs could consort with the likes of Peter Hagerman, a little rat-faced New Yorker who smoked foreign cigarettes and wore cuff links. Whenever Burroughs was angry with Peter, he began to think about Peter as his father would, which was not the way he liked to think, nor was it the way he really felt. He liked the smell of Gauloises; he liked cuff links too, but Peter's meanness often made Bud Burroughs revert to the kind of thinking he had been brought up on. Anything foreign was suspect; men, *real* men, didn't wear jewelry. There *was* a God, and J. Edgar Hoover was a good guy. The law, and not the man, was right. Bud Burroughs had been sixteen years old before he had ever even remotely entertained the idea that his father was less than perfect; he had gone a long way in three years. He had been taken part of the way by law books, when he had thought of becoming a lawyer. His literal, exacting mind had been alarmed at the capriciousness of the law; his righteous approach to justice he soon saw was grandiose, really self-righteous, even laughable. He devised a mathematical formula for getting away with murder: $OA = PM \times SL$; the opportunity for acquittal equals a plethora of money times a smart lawyer. . . . He decided on chemistry for a career.

Peter Hagerman had taken him the rest of the way. Peter was the perfect leader for Bud—cynical but rigid, sophisticated but conforming, rebellious but Republican. Burroughs, at the end of three years, saw his father objectively as an honorable, well-meaning, good-natured man overburdened with lower-class prejudices; subjectively he saw him as a clod; he happened to love him, but that could not alter the fact he *was* a clod.

It was this opinion of his father which led Burroughs to alternately worship and despise Hagerman, for Hagerman had been most influential in crystallizing this truth, so Hagerman was to be thanked for the emancipation it carried with it, and blamed, too, for the ensuing flashes of guilt.

"That's it! That's it!" Hagerman was muttering behind Burroughs. "Burroughs, you are a genius!"

Burroughs turned around and glared at Hagerman, furious at Hagerman's unrelenting self-absorption. Here was Burroughs on top of something really impressive, something he had been so eager to tell Hagerman about that he had half-run and half-walked the three miles from the lab, and there was Hagerman dancing around with his silly felt-backed clipboard, to which he attached his plans for Pi Pi's pledges.

Peter really was an adolescent; the irony was Peter thought of himself as the mature, cool member of this partnership; he thought of Bud as the wide-eyed, artless disciple.

Peter said, "Your father's gun."

"*What?*"

"I'm really out to get Shepley tomorrow. Thorpe, too, but Shepley has priority. Shepley's at the top of the list."

"Is *that* right? I had no inkling."

"Listen, Bud, neither of them knew their Divine Comedy responses. I was just down there to give them their itineraries, and neither one could get out one goddam word of the response."

"*No!*"

"Burroughs, don't get on your mother-loving high horse! I've got a bug up me, Burroughs, so don't horse around with me."

"Isn't it ever going to end? Shepley's just another guy. He's just another guy, Peter."

"Oh. Is he, Burroughs? How many other guys got their

fathers to promise the house a set of silverware if we initiated them?"

"Like Blouter said, we need the silverware, and Shepley isn't a pig, and he *is* a legacy. So what the hell?"

"Pi Delta Pi, Burroughs, is not reduced to having to take legacies!"

"Like Blouter said, if they come bearing gifts and they're not pigs, what do we have to lose?"

"Our honor."

"Come *off* it, Peter!"

"Shepley bought his way in, and he knows it!"

"He does *not* know it, Peter! His father made that damn clear; his father wouldn't want him to know it! Jesus!"

"He knew it, Bud! He was a smug bastard at Rush!"

"Shepley's an aloof type guy."

"And why, Bud? Because that mother-lover knows he can buy his way in places."

"Okay, Peter What do you have up your sleeve?"

"Your father's gun, Bud."

"Sure. Sure, Peter. I'll run over to the house and get it. It'll only take me a minute. Be sure and hold your breath while I run that little errand."

"You could get it."

"Sure. Now I'll tell one."

"Buddy, listen—this is important. I want to scare the bejesus out of Shepley. A little game of Russian roulette ought to do it, Buddy. Buddy, I don't mean we'd really leave a bullet in, but we'd make that fuckface think there was a real bullet in that gun, and Buddy, I'll bet my bird that fuckface will get down in the mud and pray for mercy. I'll bet my bird he will!"

Burroughs sighed and flopped down on his bed. He said, "In the first place, Peter, my father is never without his gun. Never! He sleeps with it under his pillow. That's a fact. You talk about *your* bird, my father would cut his off before he'd part with his gun!"

Hagerman pulled a chair up to Burroughs' bed. "Bud, never say never. When your old man takes a bath, where's his gun?"

"Peter, there are penalties for every misstep a policeman takes, and one of the biggest is the one for losing his gun."

"We'd just borrow it for a few hours."

"Be realistic, huh? You're talking about something that isn't feasible. You know me. I like to deal in facts."

"Doesn't he have more than one gun?"

"No! Now get off it!"

"I can see that I'm pushing you too far."

"I hope you can see that."

"Yeah. That's too much to ask. I can see that."

"It really is!"

"I *said* it was . . . You know me; I'm a compulsive hot-head."

"I also know you're sitting there trying to dream up a new approach to the same plan, Peter. The soft-soap approach."

Hagerman laughed. He pulled out a pack of Gauloises. "Smoke?"

"No, thanks."

Hagerman lit one for himself, sucked in the smoke, and blew out three perfectly shaped rings. After a few seconds of silence, he said, "Hey, what excited you? You never did tell me."

"My old man let me play with his gun."

"I'm serious, Bud. What was it?"

"Are you really interested, or still practicing strategy?"

"Mother-lover, you know me. It's probably a combination, but at least I'm honest."

"At least it'll change the subject, which is all I'm interested in." Burroughs sat up and faced Hagerman. "I'll take that cigarette, okay?"

Hagerman passed him one and lit it for him.

Burroughs said, "I've been experimenting at the lab, Peter. A couple of days ago I got some ergotamine tartrate and some lysergic acid. You know what I have today?"

"I hope to God you're going to say Spanish fly."

"Seriously, Peter—I've got a very good facsimile of LSD."

"Are you kidding?"

"No. I have."

"Where? Let's see it."

"It's back in the lab refrigerator. There's nothing to see. It's in some sugar cubes. It doesn't look like anything; it's what happens when you swallow it, Peter."

"Yeah. You go off your rocker."

"Wrong."

"Some guy murdered his mother-in-law when he was on the stuff, didn't he?"

"That couldn't be proved; that was a lot of yellow journalism. It's a good drug, Peter. I've read all the literature on it.

Maybe two out of two thousand have a bad reaction. The hazards are minimal."

"*Life* magazine said it made people go nuts."

"No, it *didn't!* You show me that in print anywhere, and I'll give you fifty dollars!"

"I read somewhere it makes a schizophrenic out of you."

"It *can* produce a temporary schizophrenic state; that's a slim possibility. But if you use it right, it's worth the risk. Peter, the whole world changes. It really does!"

"Drugs give me the creeps. I like the world the way it is."

"*You* don't have to try it."

"But you *are* going to try it, hmm?"

"Yes."

"It's been nice knowing you, Bud."

"Peter, I want your help. All you have to do is be with me while I do it."

"That's all, hmm? And if you should turn into a goddam nut? What happens then?"

"I won't. That's propaganda, Peter. You just feel differently, inside. Music has color and ordinary food tastes like ambrosia—it all happens inside."

"What about that little kid they took to the hospital; she was laughing and crying, half out of her mind. Remember reading about her?"

"She didn't know what was happening to her. That was an accident. Her parents didn't know anything about LSD and they got panicky. If they'd known how to handle the situation, they could have reassured the kid. It was the worst thing they could do, add to her confusion by rushing her to some hospital to have her stomach pumped out."

"Forget it, Bud. It spooks me."

"Peter, remember when we smoked marijuana last year?"

"Sure."

"It was great, wasn't it? Did it hurt us?"

"No."

"You know what the newspapers make marijuana seem like; they make it into something that sends people out to rape and steal. You know how they distort the truth. What'd we do when we had it? We sat around and giggled. Right?"

"Marijuana's different."

"So is LSD, Peter, and it's just as harmless. Sure, if some kid got ahold of marijuana and ate it and didn't know anything about it. he'd think he was off his rocker; his parents would think so, too. But when you know, you go with it, don't you? It can't scare you because you're expecting a change. LSD is the same way."

"I don't believe that, Bud."

"Put liquor into somebody who's never had any, who doesn't know how liquor affects a person. The same thing would happen."

"Marijuana can't turn you into a schizophrenic, and neither can liquor."

"Neither can LSD, Peter. The only way it can ever come close to doing that is with a particular type of person who's already unbalanced. That type could just as easily become temporarily deranged smoking pot or having a few Scotches."

"Count me out," Hagerman said. "I just don't like to mess with a drug."

"You really surprise me, Peter. You disappoint me. Remember when we first roomed together, and you used to say, 'Hey, Burroughs, take your nose out of your ass and look around. There's a big world going on, and you shouldn't miss it. You're narrow, Burroughs. You're operating with an archaic superego.' Remember, Peter? I really thought you believed that."

"I do believe that, but it's not going to turn me into a goddam dope addict."

"LSD isn't addictive."

"It spooks me, I said!"

"I'm not asking *you* to take it, am I?"

"I don't want to be party to anyone else taking it, either, you infantile son-of-a-cop!"

"And what are you, Peter? What are you? Oh. I know. You're the Pi Delta Pi Pledge Director at Far Point College. Big deal! The Pi Pi P.D. at F.P.C. Oh, that's something to *be!*"

Hagerman ground out his cigarette while his neck and face turned red. He stood up and went across to his desk, jerked out the chair and sat down with his back to Burroughs.

"Peter?"

Hagerman didn't answer.

Burroughs stood up, a thin, long-nosed, redheaded boy with pale skin and myopic brown eyes hidden behind swirls of glass. "I didn't mean that, Peter . . . It's just that I thought you'd be excited too. I wasn't at all sure I could make the stuff. It isn't as easy to make as the newspapers say it is."

Still Hagerman was silent.

Burroughs reached into the pocket of his shirt and pulled out a slip of paper. "Let me read you something, Peter. Just listen to this." He unfolded the paper. "LSD cannot be used without caution. But you can say the same thing of household ammonia, the family car, a bottle of gin, a book of matches, an oven, a paring knife, a speedboat. There are risks in everything. But the risks involved in using LSD are thought to be greater than the gains only because we have insufficient knowledge of the drug. When our ancestors had insufficient knowledge about the universe, some were against exploration and investigation of it; more were just afraid of the unknown; a few were brave enough to think man did not have to live in a cave, or starve before daring to search unknown regions for food, or die of disease before attempting treatment. There will always be, thank God, a few brave souls in any time. If man can risk a trip to the moon, why is he afraid to risk a trip into his own being? Does he believe more in the moon than in himself?"

Burroughs put the paper back in his pocket.

He said, "That was written by a doctor, Peter. An M.D."

After a small silence, Hagerman mumbled, "I wouldn't go to the moon, either."

"I didn't mean to belittle your position as Pledge Director, Peter," said Bud Burroughs. "I admire the way you take it seriously. I remember when I went through The Divine Comedy. It made a great impression on me, because you were P.D., and you took it seriously. It's just that lately I've been all fired up about the psychedelics. Peter, I really think we've got something we can't even begin to fathom, something important, something worth taking risks for."

Hagerman turned his chair around and faced Burroughs. "You really believe that, don't you?"

"I've been trying to tell you I do."

"Yes. It makes The Divine Comedy seem like small potatoes. I can see that, all right."

"Well, not exactly, but—"

"I understand."

"Do you?"

"You're right. I'm just a Pi Pi P.D. at F.P.C."

"Look, Peter, I said that like you say I'm a son-of-a-cop."

"You are . . . you are . . . But you're stretching and I'm not."

"Jesus, Peter, modesty doesn't become you."

"You've called something very important to my attention,
Bud."

"Knock it off!"

"No, you have."

"If you're going to be uncomfortable being with me while
I try the stuff, I don't want you to do it."

"I *would* be uncomfortable, Bud."

"Well. No hard feelings."

"But I think you're right about it being worth the risk.
It's just that I can't see *you* taking the risk."

"I can get someone else to be with me."

"Bud?"

"What?"

"Instead of getting someone else to be with you, while
you take the risk, let's get someone else to take the risk."

"I *want* to try it."

"Good!" said Hagerman. "And I want The Divine Comedy
to be something more than just another dumb fraternity
stunt!" Hagerman smiled. "So you take LSD *after* we see
what it does to Shepley and Thorpe."

Five

INFERNO

Canto I

(Lasciate ogni speranza, voi ch'entrate!) The South Pole of the Heavens at high noon is well above the southern horizon, and all is bathed in light. Turning north, Shepley perceives Palisades Woods. Nearest to him is Thorpe. In the heart of the forest, the pair come to a clearing, whereon they gather wood for a fire to burn ten hours. They return from whence they came.

Canto II

When the shadows of day say it is in its fourteenth hour, Shepley hears a harmonious chant: "Lamb of God, locate a portable radio, a blanket, make sandwiches, secure a jar of instant coffee." Nearest to him is Thorpe, and he perceives that he must pack it all together in preparation for a journey, north to hell.

Canto III

Shepley is roused by the sight of Hagerman's Corvair when the day is in its fifteenth hour. He descends to the curb whereupon he enters the back, wordlessly. Nearest to him is Thorpe.

PRAY FOR THEM NOW
IN THE HOUR OF THEIR NEED

When Charles Shepley finished reading his itinerary to Lois Faye, on the eve of the Inferno, he stuck the paper back inside his coat and put her pocket flashlight back in her bag. He placed the bag between them on the seat of her black Thunderbird. She drove up 9W in the rain, headed for Grandview Park. Charles had called the Bluebird Motel to reserve a room, which they would probably occupy for one hour, four hours from now, but there had been nights with her when she waited in front of the motel, with the motor running, while Charles paid for a room they never used. The clerk knew Charles; he trusted him to pay the eight dollars whether or not Charles and Lois took the room, and since the Bluebird was the only place within ten miles that never questioned a young couple, Charles was conscientious about living up to that trust.

She said, "Are you nervous about it? It sounds like a strange picnic."

"Hagerman has it in for me."

"Why?"

"I'm not rah-rah enough for him, I guess."

"I hate to drive on a night like this."

"Thorpe is really nervous. He thinks Hagerman's psychotic."

"If anything ever happened to this car, I'd never forgive myself."

"Thorpe thinks Hagerman's psychotic."

"I'd *never* forgive myself . . . You know something, Charles?"

"What?"

"You're a very lucky person."

"Why?"

"I wish things weren't so important to me."

"Things like the car?"

"Yes, things like the car."

"If I had a car, I suppose I'd worry about something happening to it."

"Oh, *you* don't know what I mean."

"Then tell me."

"Well. You don't have a car, but it doesn't bother you."
"I'd like to have a car."
"What kind?"
"I don't know. A car."
"I *begged* my family for this car."
"I suppose I wouldn't beg for one."
"I *know* you wouldn't."
"Probably not."
"But I *did!*"
"Okay, okay."
"It was important."
"I believe you."
"No you don't."
"I *do*, Lois."
"And not just any car. It had to be a 1957 Thunderbird!"
"I see."
"No you don't."
"Okay, I don't."
"I know I'm selfish."
"No, you're not selfish. What the hell."
"I am."
"I don't think you are, particularly."
"I've been told that I am, and I am!"
"All right!"
"You don't know anything about me!"
"Here's the turnoff."
"I see it."
"Well, turn off."
"No!"
"*No?*"
"No."
"Where are we going?"
"I don't know."
"Well, let me know when you decide!"
"I will."

Charles Shepley was not surprised, but he was angry, and at a loss to explain to himself just at what point in their conversation things had taken a turn for the worse. He appreciated the fact that he could seldom explain her; she worked on whim, but it did not stop him from going over whole evenings in minute detail, trying to figure out how her whims worked. He sat sideways in the seat, watching her.

He had met her his first day at Far Point College, at a

mixer. Everybody had black cards pinned to them with their names and their affiliations written across them in gold. "Independent" was written under her name, and while he talked to her, she told him Pi Phi and Kappa had both wanted her to join, but she was not a joiner. She was a short girl with long blond hair, long, thin legs, and a larger bosom than most short girls had, than most medium-sized and tall girls had, for that matter. She was a 36-C. He liked talking to her because she had a certain phony quality, which was so exaggerated it was "pop." She had a strange little accent; "no" sounded like "now"; "oh" like "ow," and near the end of the evening when she said she had to go, it sounded like: "Oy haf tew gow." Her face was glowing, because she was nervous, and her sweater was much too tight, a 34 trying to hold all that back. She had very long Fu Manchu nails, painted Certainly Red, but she wore no facial makeup except for a light pink lipstick; her eyebrows and lashes were unusually dark, and the whites of her eyes were very bright, setting off the vivid blue of her irises.

When Charles asked her if he could walk her back to the dorm, she said she would drive him to his fraternity house, and just when they were about where they were now on Route 9W, she had looked across at him and said, "You think I'm a big phony, don't you?"

"No."

"Yes you do."

Charles had said, "No," making it sound like "now."

She'd laughed. "Of course you do. I'm half-Jewish and I hate the Pi Phis and the Kappas, for they know of my tainted blood."

"You killed our Saviour."

"But you like my car, don't you?"

"Yes."

"I was born of a very wealthy family."

"Were you?"

"No."

"What else isn't true about you?"

"My last name. It isn't Faye. It's Ginzberg. But that's a secret."

"Okay."

"I don't look Jewish, do I?"

"There is no such thing as looking Jewish. Catholics don't have special physical characteristics. Methodists don't.

Seventh-Day Adventists don't. So why would those of the Jewish faith look any differently from others? . . . Did you have a nose job?"

"Yes. And it hurt, a lot."

"Do you want to go somewhere and have a drink?"

"Yes. Champagne."

The "drink" had cost Charles fifteen dollars. They had crossed the Tappan Zee bridge to Tarrytown, and gone to the bar of the Hilton Motor Inn, and while they killed the bottle of Piper Heidsieck, he had made a date with her for the next night.

Charles Shepley's allowance was fifteen dollars a week. When he got back to the Pi Pi house that night, Thorpe was asleep. His wallet was on the bureau. Charles took a ten from the bill compartment, leaving a five. It was the only time he had ever stolen in his life, but it was not the last time. In seven months, since his arrival at Far Point College, Charles had stolen $367. He had spent all of it on Lois Faye, and $120 of it had gone to the Bluebird Motel for her privilege to change her mind, which she had exercised fifteen times out of twenty-seven. Every time Charles paid for the room anyway, the Bluebird's clerk had said, "That's the way the ball bounces."

The ball was losing its resiliency; the game was wearing thin. Last month the Pi Pis had fired a Negro houseman, convinced he was the thief in their midst. The brothers were keeping their cash in the Pi Pi Mosler. Charles was spending more and more time near coat racks in campus coffee houses, and several afternoons a week wandering around the men's dorm, watching for empty rooms.

Charles kept a throw-away diary. Every day he wrote down his thoughts, read over what he had written, and promptly destroyed it. The entries were like letters from himself, keeping him up on what was happening to him. The habit had begun with the thefts; it was his way of admitting to himself what he was doing; it was there on paper, he was rational, alert to the dangers, cognizant of the fact he had no way to justify his behavior nor account for it; he logged it as one might watch the progression of a journey or an illness— but when he threw out the daily notations, and before it was time to make another entry, he dismissed it from his mind, the way his mother refused to consider herself a debtor unless she had opened the envelope containing the bill.

Last night's entry:

I told her that I would get her a Pucci blouse, which
is another thing she wants very badly. She said they
cost about fifty dollars! She said "I love Pucci and I
love Gucci." (Pocketbooks, etc.—Italian.) She must have
a huge inferiority complex. She thinks she will not be
attractive if she doesn't have the car and expensive
clothes. By the by, decided not to buy any more toilet
articles; better to lift them from the five and dime. I
got some after-shave there today; a simple operation. Got
into the faculty lounge at noon, but it netted me only
five dollars and thirty-six cents. Pi Pi is too alert to
fool much around here, but I keep my eyes open. I
must stick to dorms, restaurants, etc. I'm glad I'm not
her. It would be worse to be the one who actually must
have things like a Pucci. In conversation on phone
awhile ago I told her I owe a large gambling debt, to
prepare her for drought ahead. Cannot keep this up too
much longer without getting caught . . . The Rabbit
Hop approaches; between now and then I must get
money for rental of tux, flowers, liquor, and dinner . . .
At song fest we learned a new one with these lines:

> *"If the Chinese drop the bomb*
> *Or I'm sent to Vietnam,*
> *I'll still feel blessed.*
> *If a Pi Pi pin is on my chest,*
> *I'll still feel blessed.*
> *If I have to die,*
> *Let my last words be Pi Pi."*

Hagerman was so moved he had tears in his eyes; I pretended to drop something, bumped against him, got his
gold lighter from his sweater pocket, but it has Pi
Pi crest on it, damn! Who'd buy that?

Lois Faye said, "What are you thinking about?"
"I wasn't thinking. I was watching the road."
"Watching us get farther and farther away from the park,
huh?"
"Yes."
"You're angry, aren't you?"
"Yes."

"Disappointed, even heartsick?"

"What's the matter with you? I wonder about you."

"Aren't you disappointed, even heartsick?"

"Yes."

"Why?"

"You know damn well why!"

"Why? Was going to the park so important?"

"It was to me."

"It was that important?"

"Yes, it was that important."

"And you're seething inside, aren't you? Your stomach's in knots."

"You're so right."

"I know I am. I just wanted you to have some idea of how *I* felt before I got this car."

"*What?*"

"It's awful, Charles, isn't it, when something's important and you can't have it?"

"You're sick, Lois. Did you ever think of that?"

"Am I too ill to go to the park?"

"Oh, my God!" and he began to laugh.

She laughed too. She said, "Tell me when you see some place I can turn around."

One night Charles had double-dated with Thorpe. Pi Pi pledges were required to date four sorority girls a month, during their first semester of membership. That particular night Thorpe and Charles had taken two Tri Delts to Grand-view Park in Thorpe's Chevrolet. Thorpe had taken his date into the woods for a walk, while Charles sat in the back seat with his. She was not a good conversationalist, and she did not smoke; Tri Delt pledges were forbidden to drink. Charles could think of little to do with her but kiss her. He did, and she kissed him back, and there was a lot of tongue involvement, and she let him put his hands up under her sweater and unhook her brassiere, all within the first half hour. In the second half hour when Charles moved his hand down, she took his hand away, and he put it back, and she took it away, and he put it back, and finally she said, "No, really."

"Okay," he said.

He smoked a cigarette and complained about having a Saturday class, and she said she was glad she didn't have one, and then he put his cigarette out and began all over again, minus step three, since he could tell she meant no to that. But he thought of other things while he was kissing her and touching her breasts, and he wished Thorpe would come back, and he remembered Lois. He had been home the weekend before, and he had visited his father's lab at the Richmond Institute, where his father was involved in an elaborate research project involving the mating habits of invertebrate animals. The lab was lighted only by the artificial daylight lamps in the breeding cases; it was a beautiful effect, green and still and shadowy. He had stood quietly and observed the peculiar fluttering flight of a silver-washed fritillary, with the male in close pursuit, gliding around in rings, as she alighted on a large red flower and spread her wings so wide they lay quite flat, and then he had moved on and watched two dragonflies nestle on the tip of a reed. The female curved her belly into the male, sliding in between his feet, lifting herself gently toward his chest, while they moved very subtly and sensitively together; then they were nearly immobile save for the tiniest fluttering of the male's wings, and the contractions of his threadlike abdomen.

His father had remarked, "Human intercourse seems so clumsy in contrast to this, so lacking in grace."

Charles had nodded in agreement, but he had been with Lois Faye by that time, and he had thought that however volatile and unpredictable she was, however much it cost in dollars and patience and strategy to get her to the room at the Bluebird, however drunk they always were by the time they did get there, it was never ordinary or awkward; it was always graceful and natural and good.

"Charles?" the Tri Delt pledge had whispered to him, while he was touching her breasts on the second go-round that night in the back of Thorpe's Chevy, "Charles?"

He had stopped and asked, "What?"

She had tapped him on the tip of his nose with her finger, smiled coquettishly, and said, "Hello."

Well, maybe she had no feeling in her breasts.

There had been a girl Charles had dated in high school, who always giggled when Charles touched her there: "I can't *help* it! It tickles," and another who gently reproved him once, "Too much of that can hurt like the dickens!" But Lois would look into his eyes very solemnly and say, "I won't be able to stop you from doing anything you want to do to me if you keep that up," which was not true, because she usually stopped him soon after she said it, if she were going to talk at all at a time like that, but he did not feel angry or foolish or clumsy; she was not an artless girl in any situation.

What they did in the park was listen to the songs on the radio and drink and talk; that was 85 percent of it; the 15 percent, the kissing and all that, came at the very end, the last half hour; it was their pre-Bluebird ritual, though there was no guarantee that Charles would get her to go with him to the motel each time. There were times (two) when she had astonished him by saying, "Can we go to the Bluebird?" as though he had not called in advance to reserve the room, and times when they had long arguments in front of the Bluebird, until Charles gave up and got out of the car only long enough to pay for the room; and there were the times he won the arguments, despite her insistence that she had to go back to the dorm immediately ("Now, oy haf to gow!"), when they would leave before closing hour at the dorm, and she would drop him off at Pi Pi, and blow him a kiss, and give her horn a little honk as she drove away, and he would go inside drugged with love, wondering what he could steal next.

She drank Southern Comfort, because she hated the taste of most hard liquor, and he drank the worst kind of house brand rotgut, which he always poured into a pint bottle of Haig and Haig, and the conversation began pretty much the way it did that night.

"The third song that plays after this one, has a special message for you." Nancy Sinatra was singing "Boots" and the rain was falling against the windshield and splashing over the roof, and they had cigarettes going and shot glasses they had stolen from the 76 House in Old Tappan, for their drinks.

"A message about what?"

"The kind of man you'll marry."

" 'Daddy,' " she sang, " 'I want a diamond ring, champagne, everything—' "

"Wait and see what it is," he said; they played this game over and over: the messages from songs. She sighed and wound her violet chiffon scarf around her hand and said, "You don't even know where to buy a Pucci, do you?"

"In New York."

"Where?"

"At their store."

"See? You *don't* know! They don't have a store!"

"You said they had one on Fifth Avenue."
"That's Gucci! You're really thick!"
"Okay, that's Gucci."
"You don't even know what they sell!"
"Leather. Pocketbooks."
"Pocketbooks? Where did you get that word?"
"Pocketbooks?"
"You don't say that anymore. You say purse or handbag."
"Oh."
"You're really a hick."
"Where do I get a Pucci then?"
"You won't get me one. I know that."
"I said I would."
"I wouldn't accept it. It's too much money."
"That's for me to decide."
"You can get them at Sak's Fifth Avenue."
"Them? How many do you want?"
"Lots! I want lots of everything expensive . . . Charles?"
"What?"
"Do you think I'm grabby?"
"No."
"Yes I am."
"Okay, you are."
"I've been told that I am, and I am."
"Did you ever see spiders mate?"
"No."
"I watched these Pisauras when I was home, at my dad's lab. The male would take a fly and spin it into a round lump, and then he'd carry it with his chelicerae to the female. He'd be—"
"Is that what you're going to be?"
"What?"
"A zoologist like your father?"
"I don't know yet . . . Anyway, the male spider would carry the fly up to the female, with his hind end shaking and his feelers out, and she'd just sit there and watch him. And he'd be all worked up, and he'd present her with the fly, and *pffft*, she'd scramble away. The damn fly would fall, and the spider would have to go after another one. Eventually, the female would accept it, and then while she was eating it, he'd hop on her; but it all worked on whim. Her whim."
"Do you *like* bugs?"
"It's interesting work. My dad's lab is one of the most beautiful rooms I've ever seen. These breeding cases are all

lit up, and there're a lot of green plants inside that make shadows on the white walls, and instead of a phone ringing, which would disturb things—the noise would distract—there's a blue light that flashes when a call comes through."

"I hate my father for being a dentist."

"I'd love you to see the lab."

"I'd like to see it."

"Would you really?"

"Yes."

"You know, I think you'd be fascinated by some of the experiments. Do you know, there are some Mexican lizards which reproduce themselves without male partners. What's their name again? It's on the tip of my tongue. They're about ten inches long, very quick-moving lizards. Their way of reproducing themselves is called parthenogenesis. The egg's developed from a virgin female without fertilization by spermatozoa."

"You know a lot about zoology, don't you?"

"Sure. My dad brought me up on it. My brother wasn't interested in it. Parthenogenesis isn't as rare as you might think. Certain insects and—"

She said, "What does he do, just lie there all day?"

"Who?"

"Your brother."

"He's a vegetable. He just lies there. Certain insects and crustaceans and worms reproduce themselves—"

"It's depressing," she said. "Doesn't it depress you?"

"I don't think about it."

"If anything like that ever happened to me, I wouldn't want to live."

"You wouldn't know the difference. He doesn't know the difference. Let me tell you about these lizards. What's their name? It's on the tip of my—"

"Here's my song, Charles! Listen!"

> He's a real nowhere man,
> Sitting in his nowhere land
> Making all his nowhere plans
> For nobody.

She said, "Turn the dial. I hate it!"

"You know something about that song? My roommate—"

"Please! Turn the dial, Charles!"

"If you'd just listen a minute, I'll tell you something very funny that Dan Thorpe did with this song and—"

"No! It's a depressing song, and you said it had a special message for me!"

Charles turned the dial; he got Nancy Wilson singing "More."

"That's better, isn't it?" he said.

"I'm nowhere."

"Oh, stop, Lois."

"I'm a real nowhere girl, going nowhere. I'll probably end up in the suburbs going to Hadassah meetings."

Charles laughed.

"Don't laugh. It's not a bit funny! Do you think I'll meet any rich men *here?*"

"*I'm* going to buy you a Pucci," Charles smiled.

"No you're not. I know you're not."

"I've never broken a promise to you yet."

"I'm nowhere, and I'm making nowhere plans for nobody."

"The name of that lizard is Cnemidophorus tessellatus. I just thought of it. Cnemidophorus tessellatus."

"I wish I were like you, Charles."

"Why?"

"You don't care. It doesn't bother you not to have things."

"I'll get you things. Then it won't bother you. Okay?"

She gave him one of her wistful smiles and put her cigarette out the window. She looked at him a moment, and then she said, "What's taking you so long to touch me."

Charles smiled back while his stomach flipped. "I thought it was too early."

She said, "It isn't."

He started to reach for her, but she caught his hands in hers, brought them to her lips, and said, "Not here." She kissed his hands and put them back in his lap. "We'll go to the bluebird of happiness."

"All right," Charles said, trying to sound cool.

She started the car. "Do you like Nancy Wilson?" she said.

"Yes."

"So do I. This is a pretty song. 'More.' "

"Very!" Charles agreed.

They swung onto the winding road leading out of Grand-view Park.

She said, "But I do not like lizards. I like Barbra

Streisand, and I like the dress I'm going to wear to the Rabbit Hop. It's a Dior."

"Is it?" She was probably crazy, Charles decided.

"No."

"What's it like?"

She told him, in great detail, while he sat watching the rain, trying to contain his excitement. He sneaked a look at his wristwatch, wary now of anything he did or said, for fear she would change her mind. It was only quarter to nine, the earliest they had ever been to the motel; that gave them three and a half hours. Dazzled, Charles shut his eyes and saw on the screen of his thoughts all they would do, heard all they would say, and planned to pick up his stereophonic phonograph when he went home for Easter Sunday, stay on until Monday to sell it, and buy the Pucci before he came back. . . . That still left a good day's work finding the money for the Rabbit Hop, and tomorrow was the start of the damn Divine Comedy. He decided to try and hit the Coke machines and laundromats in the Pi Pi basement when he got back to the house; they would probably be good for fifteen or twenty dollars, if he could get into them.

When they pulled into the Bluebird and stopped before the office, she put her hand on Charles's arm as he was about to get out and pay the clerk. "No!"

"No?"

"You heard me."

"Don't pull this, Lois. My God!"

"Can't *I* pay for a change?"

"What?"

"For you have a gambling debt." she said. Then she opened the door on her side and got out, and walked through the rain to the entrance of the office.

Dumbstruck, Charles watched while she stood at the counter inside, and opened her handbag, and passed bills across to the man. She had the flimsy, violet-colored chiffon scarf over her hair, and a shaggy llama coat, and the smell of her perfume, Celui, was there in the car.

During those few moments, Charles Shepley fell in love with her.

When she got back inside the car, she said, "Here's a quarter for the ice machine."

She pressed the quarter into his palm. "You prefer your Scotch with ice, don't you?"

"Yes."

"We're in Number Six, Charles. Watch for Six. I think I ran a stocking."

"Six," he managed.

The radio played while Charles fixed his drink in the glass from the bathroom, and she hung up her dress on a hanger. She sat on the bed, in her slip and stockings and heels, and lit two cigarettes, one for Charles. He took it and sat on the footstool near the bed, not to hurry things; he didn't take off his tie or his coat. He would do it all at once in the bathroom before a quick shower. It was a sticky, warm March night.

She said, "Don't you want to sit here?" patting the bed.

"Sure."

He moved up and sat beside her, almost touching but not touching.

She said, "I like this tacky old place. I always have."

"So have I."

"Even the stains on the wallpaper."

"Yes, even that."

"You're very good for me, aren't you, Charles?"

"I hope I am."

"You are, you know."

She took his hand again; she brought it up and put it near her neck, rubbing her chin against it. When she let go of it, he put his arms around her and for a long time they kissed. He slipped the straps of her bra down and touched her and both of them were getting excited; she was catching her breath and whispering "oh" and murmuring "sssssss" and finally Charles told her, "I'll be right back."

"Shall I fix you another drink?"

"That's still pretty new, but thanks."

"Do you think you'll *love* the dress I wear to the Rabbit Hop?"

"Yes. I'll love it."

"I know you will. You'll love it a lot. It's a very expensive Balenciaga purchased for me at great cost by my wealthy family."

Charles laughed, "I'll be out in a second."

"And I have many, many like it," she said, "I have tons of Norells and Balenciagas and St. Laurents and—name it!"

He was not going to take a shower. He stripped off his clothes and wiped his body with a wet towel, soaping his hands and face and under his arms, and rinsing off his feet.

As he dried himself he decided he would cut off his legs for her; anything . . . *anything.*

He wrapped a clean towel around his waist, combed his hair, and gave his reflection a smile and a wink.

The room was empty.

He went to the door and called her name. Then he saw that the car was gone.

There was a note on the bed.

This here Pisaura spider scrambled down the web— pffft—and ran away. What do you know about that?

She had even spelled Pisaura right.

Charles Shepley fell face down on the bed, and pounded the pillow with his fist.

Six

"Every pledge in the place is signed out for Easter Sunday," said Hagerman.

Burroughs only nodded. He was sitting on his bed in his Hawaiian Perma-prest pajamas, holding a tube of Crest and his Py-Co-Pay, but not making a move to go down the hall and use them. Hagerman knew he was still brooding over their plans for Shepley and Thorpe the next day; Hagerman wanted to get off that subject before Bud changed his mind, and ruined the Inferno.

The four sugar cubes which Bud had brought from the lab were sitting on Hagerman's desk, wrapped in aluminum foil. The Pi Pi refrigerator was kept locked to prevent raiding parties, but Hagerman had his own key. Mother Varner had given him one, so he could keep his medicine there. He kept it in a pigskin Mark Cross zipper case; there was a lock on that too. Hagerman never said what his medicine was, beyond the fact that it was for his nerves. He would rather die than admit that the case contained Compazine suppositories. They were tranquilizers, not laxatives—that was some comfort—but Hagerman was one of those people who would often allow himself to become constipated rather than use the bathroom when others were using it; he was the sort who had managed to make anything to do with that part of his body into a taboo that loomed as large in his thoughts as sex did in the thoughts of an adolescent boy. He seldom used the Pi Pi john; he drove in search of Shell signs and the flying red horse, and he frequented the seedy rest rooms of road stands and sandwich shops. He suffered from bouts of colitis and hid tubes of Preparation H under his socks in his bureau. On bad nights he worried that he had cancer and a colostomy would be performed on him. The only one who knew his guilty secret was Burroughs, to whom he had made a drunken confession. He had regretted it ever since. On rare occasions when Burroughs did not accept Hagerman's word as gospel, Hagerman took that thread and wove it into a tapestry depicting Burroughs' growing disrespect for Hagerman, dating back to that rainy afternoon downstairs in the Pi Pi Pub, when Hagerman had whispered the truth about his physical condition.

Burroughs seldom crossed Hagerman, though; if he lost his temper with Hagerman, he was quick to pacify him minutes later, and in the process of pacification, to make promises he would not normally make. That was the situation Hagerman had him in that night; that accounted for the dejection, the mutism, the unbrushed teeth, and for Hagerman's desire to get Burroughs' mind off the sugar cubes on the desk, onto anything that might propel him back to the routine tasks of an evening and allow Hagerman to secure the treated sweets in his Mark Cross case downstairs.

Said Hagerman, "Most of the actives are signed out for Easter Sunday, too."

A grunt for an answer.

"That doesn't surprise me, but it does surprise me about the pledges."

"Uh-huh."

"We don't have that many from around here. Just Shepley and Kent and Gaelen."

"Ummm."

"The rest are all from New England or the Midwest. They've all found a place to go, though."

"Ummm."

"Is it a big day at your house?"

Burroughs only shrugged.

Hagerman said, "I haven't figured out what I'm going to do."

Burroughs had never asked Hagerman to his house; he lived right in Far Point, a ten-minute drive from the college, and he went home every Sunday, and sometimes for dinner on a week night, but he had never suggested that Hagerman come along. It had been Hagerman who had gotten him into Pi Delta Pi. The fraternity was not at all keen on "townies." Townies were invariably druggists' sons or opticians' sons or sons of Thom McAn shoe salesmen; they did nothing to enhance the fraternity in the eyes of National. National liked a good geographical distribution, as well; National was always after its local chapters to "put a pin in every state."

What had impressed Hagerman about Burroughs was Burroughs' eagerness. The style these days at Rush was to play it cool—not quite as cool as someone like Shepley might play it, but loose, unruffled; you didn't walk around saying, "Gee, this is a *great* house!" as Burroughs had when he'd gone through Rush; you said, "Nice place," if you were going to say anything at all—never, "This is the best house I've seen," as Burroughs had, because that told anyone that the Dekes were not rushing you. The other frat houses were outhouses compared to the Dekes' palace on Palisades Road.

But Hagerman argued before the brothers that a fraternity needed men who were really impressed by it; such men sparked a fraternity; they were the men who volunteered for the prosaic offices like Treasurer, Recording Secretary, Housemother Escort, "and," Hagerman had finished dramatically, "Pledge Director. I am proud to say that I was every bit as enthusiastic as Burroughs when I came up that Pi Pi walk for the first time. And it'll be the likes of me, and a Burroughs, who'll send our checks to National long after we've gone down that front sidewalk for the last time!"

Burroughs had demonstrated his gratitude to Hagerman in every way possible but that one: asking him to his house.

Hagerman was not surprised; he was always riding Burroughs about being a son-of-a-cop, but Hagerman was secretly angry with Burroughs for not realizing that Peter Hagerman, were he ever asked to Burroughs' house, would be charm incarnate.

Hagerman had never asked Burroughs home with him either; it was a thirty-minute drive across the George Washington Bridge, down the West Side Highway, and across to Sutton Place. There, in a three-story yellow-brick town house with tan shutters and an attached garage which housed a green Morgan, Leonard Hagerman held forth on the virtues of Hagerman Advertising Incorporated, which boiled down every time to a testimonial to Golden Boy himself. Old Len. Len Lovely, the Man.

Peter Hagerman had a little weasel face with beady eyes which were too close together, very small lips which were practically not there at all, and the kind of complexion yellow journalists often attributed to sex fiends—red-faced. His father had one of those faces which showed everything he was thinking, and sometimes when he looked at Peter, when he deigned to look at Peter, Hagerman could tell his old man was wondering how a handsome son-of-a-bitch like himself had ever spawned such a nebbish.

Hagerman had spent last weekend at Old Len's and Peg Beauty's, and near midnight of that Saturday, Len Lovely had cracked the Greek tourist account nut with another hot Hagerman special, in honor of which he had popped open a bottle of Mumm's to toast his creation. He had swept into the observatory room, the room where he kept his telescope, and while Peter and his mother sat on the window seat waiting for the unveiling, he had clutched a piece of large white cardboard to him, and delivered a ten-minute lecture on how hard his work was and how impossible it would really be for him to excel without their support. *Their* support. There were not two of Hagerman's mother. But he was a big man, Len Lovely, and a generous man, and his son was sitting right there; he must have figured he could afford to include the creep. It *was* Academy Award night, after all, wasn't it? He had just won an Oscar, right?

Peg Beauty said, "Please show us, Len!"

Len the Man said, "In a minute, in a minute—"

"Please, Len!"

"In a minute!"

"Dying!"

"One . . . two . . . *three!*"

And there it was: a huge white space with a little tiny picture of the Acropolis in the center, and in big bold letters the word:

GREECEMARK

Underneath, the legend:

GREECE WILL LEAVE ITS MARK ON YOU
IT WON'T RUB OUT!

There was applause from Peg Beauty, and Hagerman managed a smile and a "Good," and Peg Beauty rushed into Len

Lovely's arms and planted noisy kisses on his cheeks and mouth and neck.

"Do you really like it, Peg?"

"Oh, Len, yes. Yes!"

"I think I targeted right in on it."

"You did. You targeted right in on it."

"Greecemark. Greece will leave its mark on you. It won't rub out. Should it be 'it won't *come* out'?"

"No rub. Rub's perfect."

"It won't rub out."

"It won't rub out."

"Greece will leave its mark on you. It won't rub out."

"Greecemark! Beautiful, Len."

"You really like it?"

"I swear. I swear. It's stunning."

"I think it says it."

"It does."

"Greecemark."

"Greece will leave its mark on you. It won't rub out."

Hagerman never would ask Burroughs home with him either, for fear Burroughs might ask, "Are you *sure* you live here?"

Last Sunday as Hagerman was leaving Old Len's and Peg Beauty's, Peg Beauty had said, "I'm giving a big party for your father at the Sign of the Dove next Sunday. He deserves a reward."

In the second that followed, Peter Hagerman decided first to refuse to attend, and then to what-the-hell accept.

Then his mother said, "Enjoy your Easter, darling."

Hagerman lit a cigarette and went across the room to retrieve Ursula Andress from the wastebasket, where she stood clutching her pistols. He carried it over to the wall and began pushing the nail attached to it back into the hole. "I've never really understood all the fuss over Easter," he said.

Burroughs was like a dummy; he just sat there, frowning.

Hagerman said, "Guys like Blouter flying all the way to Saint Louis. Would you fly all the way to Saint Louis for Easter?"

"Hmmm?"

"I said, would you fly all the way to Saint Louis for Easter? Blouter flew all the way to Saint Louis."

"I don't know . . . I might . . . Listen, Peter, I don't want to go through with it."

Hagerman had been waiting for this, steeling himself against this.

"You made a promise, Bud."

"I don't feel right about it. We don't have the right set-setting for one thing."

"Don't be an old maid, Bud."

"The set-setting is very important. I explained that to you, Peter. Set and setting determine the direction of the whole LSD experience."

"Let's not get bogged down in the jargon, Bud. . . . There . . . your girl friend's back up on the wall."

"Thanks, but it won't work. You're so damn obvious, Peter!"

"Why won't it work? You said you'd agree if we had a controlled situation. Now, Buddy, I promised you we'll do it up real nice for the boys. Didn't I set it up like a picnic? Didn't I? We'll have a campfire and music and a quiet spot —hell, they'll have themselves a ball."

"You don't believe that for a minute."

"*You* convinced me."

"Sure I did. . . . Peter, it *can* be a dangerous drug. If *I* take it, that's one thing: I know what to expect, but Shepley and Thorpe don't know anything about it!"

"We agreed to tell them, right? We'll tell them as soon as it's down inside their little tum-tums. 'Fellows, that was not just soda pop you drank; that was an elixir which will turn you on as you have never before been turned on, so fasten your seat belts, gentlemen, you are about to take a trip.' "

Burroughs groaned. "It just isn't funny, Peter."

"I won't clown it up when we get there. I'll be as serious as a priest. I'll be Timothy Leary, I promise. I'll be Aldous Huxley, I give you my word."

"No . . . I can't give it to them unless they want to take it."

"Well, they're not goint to *want* to take it, Bud! Use your head, Buddy! They're probably as brainwashed as I was about LSD before *you* enlightened me, hmmm?"

Sometimes when Hagerman soft-soaped Burroughs, he was amazed at how gullible Bud was, and they were the times he felt tender toward him, as though it were all right for him to put Bud on, but he would kill anyone else who took advantage of Bud's ingenuous nature; other times, not many, but times like this, when Bud seemed strong, Hagerman felt the beginnings of a landslide inside him, the first stirrings of something loosening, about to give, and his heartbeat seemed to pound right into his flesh, because he expected it from others, but not from Bud. He had stood up in chapter meeting and fought to get Bud in Pi Pi; he had gone way out on a limb for that boy, way out on a goddam twig.

Burroughs said, "I didn't enlighten you. You still think the way you did; you're just hoping for the worst. . . . It's off, Peter."

"Bud, you made a promise."

"I can't keep it."

"Thanks, Bud. I'll remember this. I'll remember this for a long time."

"You'd have worse memories if something went wrong tomorrow."

"You said nothing could go wrong! You SAID that!"

"I meant if *I* take it, Peter."

"You SAID we could do it if we had a controlled SITUATION!"

"It isn't controlled if they don't know what they're taking *before* they take it."

"What the HELL am I supposed to DO with them tomorrow?"

"You talk about control. *Look* at you. Jesus!"

"I CARE about The Divine Comedy!"

"If you do, think it through. What do you think Blouter will say when they tell him that we gave them LSD?"

"They wouldn't tell Blouter. They wouldn't go running to Blouter like little tattletales."

"You're not thinking, Peter. If their trip didn't turn out well, they'd sure as hell high-tail it to Blouter. Peter, I can't get it across to you, can I? A lot of things could go wrong. For instance, Peter," Burroughs stood up and waved his Py-Co-Pay to make his point, "we don't know if a hundred and fifty micrograms is too much or too little. There's a hundred and fifty micrograms of the stuff in each one of those sugar cubes. I say that's about right for me, but I'm only guessing. If I were going to give LSD to you, I'd give you less—about a hundred micrograms—because you're smaller than I am. Don't you see? It's not a simple matter."

"Shepley and Thorpe are your size."

"Their tolerance could still be different; their dispositions are different. Shepley's the quiet type; we don't know what the hell goes on inside Shepley. Thorpe's got a thing about his body—did you ever see him put sun lotion on himself, up on the roof? He's a narcissist or something. Peter, don't you get it? The stuff does strange things to people, particularly people who don't know beans about it! Thorpe could think something was happening to his body—he'd go ape, Peter! He'd go ape if that happened. He hasn't got anything to go by that'll help him understand what would happen to him; neither has Shepley. I wasn't thinking, Peter. Can't you accept that? I just wasn't thinking when I agreed to this."

"You really think they'd tell Blouter?"

"If you were a pledge and someone give you LSD without telling you what you were taking, wouldn't you kick up a hailstorm?"

"The HELL I WOULD!"

"Okay, Peter. *You* wouldn't. You'd let somebody bury you in a shithouse for old Pi D Pi, but not many other guys would."

Hagerman went across and sat down at his desk. Burroughs knew what strings to work. Blouter was something else. How Blouter had ever come to be the president of Pi Delta Pi, Hagerman had never appreciated. because it was common knowledge that Blouter was a cynical bastard who had not even invested in a jeweled pin, but there were few real Greeks left—Hagerman did appreciate that; Hagerman was one of them, maybe the only ardent one in Pi Pi, and now Burroughs had touched on something Hagerman could not pass over lightly. It was one thing for Shepley and Thorpe to go ape for eight hours; it was another for them to go to Blouter afterward. The president of a fraternity had the authority to recommend deactivation; it was almost never done, yet Blouter had come close to doing it to Hagerman last semester when Hagerman had disciplined a pledge named Osmond.

Osmond was one of those pledges like Shepley, one of those above-it-all characters who thought the words to the frat songs were silly and who always had a real put-upon expression whenever he participated in fraternity rituals. Hagerman had caught him making fun of the Candlelight Ceremony which Pi Pi held the third Sunday of every month; this was Hagerman's favorite Pi Pi rite, during which the brothers sang "Pi Pi, My Love for You is Why I Strive," standing in a circle, hands joined in the secret

Pi D Pi grip. Hagerman had come upon Osmond doing a lisping burlesque of it before a roomful of pledges, mincing around and carrying the gold Pi Pi loving cup upside down on his head. So Hagerman had suspended his weekend privileges, despite the fact Osmond's mother was in critical condition in a New York hospital. When Osmond had tried to bolt out the back door of the house, Hagerman had gotten another pledge's help, and locked Osmond down in the pub, with a gag across his mouth and his arms and legs tied.

Most of the house was at Rutter Field watching F.P.C. play Fairleigh Dickinson that afternoon; Osmond had worked himself free in a few hours and hollered and banged on the pub door until a houseboy let him out. But his mother had been dead for an hour by then.

Osmond went to pieces; that night Blouter had him up on Three in the president's suite, and Pi Pis and their dates heard Osmond's wailing and cussing all the way to the front porch. A day later Osmond depledged and left Far Point; Blouter began proceedings against Hagerman.

Blouter had said, "Hagerman, didn't it ever dawn on you that one of the reasons Osmond couldn't take it all very seriously was that something *really* serious was affecting his life?"

That was Blouter in a nutshell; that was the way Blouter thought. First, wet-nurse the pledges. First, let anyone join whose old man could cough up a set of silverware. First, pick out the cheapest Pi Pi pin Balfour sold. First, fly all the way to St. Louis, Missouri, on the eve of The Divine Comedy. . . . Second, think of Pi Delta Pi.

Bud Burroughs took his towel off the rack on the back of his closet door and pushed his feet into slippers. "I just wasn't thinking, Peter," he said. "I'll help you come up with something else to do to Shepley and Thorpe."

"Nobody helps me come up with ideas for The Divine Comedy, Burroughs. I've been coming up with ideas for The Divine Comedy for three years running, *by myself!*"

"I didn't mean it that way; I just meant that maybe together we could kick it around, and you'd come up with something."

"You know what that son-of-a-bitch was doing the other night at song fest, Burroughs?"

"Who?"

"Shepley! He dropped something, see? And we were right

in the middle of 'I'll Feel Blessed.' And that son-of-a-mother-lover bent right over and picked it up."

"Yeah," said Burroughs. "Well . . . ." and he carried his toothpaste and toothbrush toward the door, pausing before he left the room to say, "Put the stuff in the refrigerator, Peter. I'll take it back to the lab tomorrow."

Hagerman said, "He couldn't wait for the end of the song. That's how much the song meant to him."

It was eleven thirty; in fifteen more minutes all females except Mother Varner were to be out of the Pi D Pi house. Because it was a rainy night, there were more there than usual. Hagerman could hear the hi-fi blasting in the first-floor date room, and he knew that the kitchen was probably filled with men fetching last cups of coffee for their dates before seeing them home.

Hagerman decided to wait until the house was cleared of women before putting away the sugar cubes. He was not shy with women; he had a very easy manner around women and they liked him, but he did not date and he felt conspicuous when he went down to the pub and everyone else was there with a date, or when he came up the front sidewalk late in the evening and the front porch was filled with couples. At Pi Pi dances, at exchange dinners, at holiday parties, Hagerman always volunteered to act as Mother Varner's escort.

The story on Hagerman was common knowledge; he was pinned to a Gamma Phi who attended Ohio State. Her father would not allow her to fly, so Hagerman always had to go to her, which he managed four or five times a school year. The rest of the time Hagerman was busy writing her; long, long letters, composed at his desk, which contained a large gold-framed photograph of her with the inscription, "For Peter, my man, in every sense of the word, with deepest love, Janice."

It had gotten so that even Hagerman believed the story, though not enough to actually mail those long, long letters or hop a plane to Columbus. He mailed very short notes to his cousin, and while he was supposed to be rendezvousing with her some thousand miles away from Far Point, he was actually only thirty minutes away, in his room at Len Lovely's and Peg Beauty's, sacked out or reading or watching TV.

But he did believe enough in the story to write very authentic letters, which were always lying around on his desk for anyone to read, and he believed enough to enjoy writing the letters, to collect himself writing them, so that was what he did in that fifteen-minute interval, while he waited for the girls to leave the house.

> My dearest Janice,
> Thank you for your very loving letter.

It was Hagerman's luck that his cousin was one of those silly girls who wrote an answer to a letter the same day she received it; she dotted her *i*'s with little stars and enclosed Ohio State stickers and rattled on about nothing at all, never finding anything odd in the fact that it was Cousin Peter she was writing at the rate of six or seven letters a month, although the few times she and Cousin Peter had ever been in each other's company were as colorful as a sack of flour.

> I don't think I could continue without your loyal support.

Shades of Len Lovely; an apple never falls far from the tree.

> I wish you would not worry so about me, my darling. Believe me, I am wearing my rubbers when it rains and my scarf when it snows and my heart, always, on my sleeve.

Yyikh!

> Janice, I am happy to know that you feel about Gamma Phi, as I do about Pi Delta Pi. We are old-fashioned, I suppose, anachronisms in a world that no longer cherishes tradition, honor, integrity. Only today I learned that our president decided to skip off to St. Louis, at the very start of The Divine Comedy. He may be popular (he is), he may be admired (he appears to be), but he will never have my respect, for he does not respect the high office of Pi Delta Pi honored him with. When he ordered his pin, he not only chose the cheapest, he also did not bother to order the little gold gavel, which the president of a fraternity may attach to his pin. Every other president of a fraternity on this campus wears a gavel on his pin (I checked this out)

but our president apparently does not think highly enough of his position to invest in one.

Then too, there is the matter of Easter Sunday, a day of absolutely no importance to me, yet our young pledges from out of state have had to wheedle their ways into the homes of brothers who live nearby, for Pi Pi is not even serving Sunday dinner on that day. It seems to me—

Hagerman stopped writing at the sound of the 11:45 bell. He was definitely more nervous than usual; he was eager to get a Compazine inside of him. The letter-writing had not calmed him down at all, and he felt the beginnings of a vast depression rolling in, first in nagging ripples of anxiety, and then in great swells of something akin to terror.

It had not done Hagerman any good to remember the way Blouter had humiliated him by forcing him to beg for another chance after the Osmond episode. This was the crux of Hagerman's fright, but this mushroomed into puffs of tension that had to do now with Burroughs' lack of respect for Hagerman, because Hagerman was the victim of an ugly illness which might well be cancer; and then it had to do with Len Lovely, who always walked down a street a little ahead of Peter, as though he were not with him; now Blouter en route to St. Louis, without even asking Hagerman what he had planned for The Divine Comedy ("Just go easy on them, Peter; they're our pledges, not our enemies."); then Shepley bending down to pick up something during "I'll Feel Blessed"; Thorpe then, on his bed in his drawers, listening to some smart-ass song that laughed at men who were dedicated; then Osmond with the gold loving cup upside down on his head, making a mockery of a ceremony which often left Hagerman teary-eyed; now Inferno itineraries for Shepley and Thorpe that were useless unless Hagerman could think of something fantastic, something as horrible as he had threatened.

"What's eating you, Peter?"

Brushed Teeth was back from the john.

"There's nothing *eating* me, Burroughs."

"No? You look like somebody just took a chunk out of your middle."

"Burroughs, I'm holding my stomach because I have a pain there. I suppose that's amusing, is it? I suppose that gives you a big yak!"

"How was I supposed to know?"

"Because I explained MY CONDITION TO YOU!"

"Okay. Okay. Jesus! Get a hold of yourself."

"I don't need your respect. You don't have mine and I don't need yours."

"What'd you do, take one of those sugar cubes? You sound like you're off your stick, Peter." Then Burroughs grinned at Hagerman. "Oh, look, Peter, you just miss Janice. That's all that's eating you."

Sometimes Hagerman was truly grateful for Burroughs' simple-mindedness. Or did the credit really belong to Peter Hagerman for having the wits to survive somehow, in a jungle of animals where fraternity meant little more than a place to sleep and eat and use the toilet?

"I'll lock up the explosives," said Hagerman. He smiled back at Burroughs, and put the sugar cubes in the pocket of his official blue and white wool Pi Delta Pi robe, with the gold crest stitched above his heart.

The Pi Delta Pi phone room was on the first floor of the house; Hagerman had to pass it to reach the kitchen. It was a room built especially for long distance calls; it was the size of a bathroom, with a glass door, a comfortable leather chair, phone books from all over the country, and a sign on the wall which read:

THIS ROOM FOR LONG DISTANCE CALLS ONLY.
DO NOT USE FOR ANY OTHER CALLS WITHOUT PERMISSION.

There were two extensions to the phone, one on the second floor and another on the third, but they were open phones which afforded no privacy; when a Pi Pi called his family, he used this room.

As Hagerman passed by, he looked in and saw Charles Shepley. Shepley was standing there in a wet raincoat with his back to Hagerman. Hagerman could just imagine a conversation of Shepley's with his family; he could just imagine the carrying-on: Did you wear your rubbers today, Charles? It was raining. Did you get the check Daddy sent you, Charles? Do you need more? Charles, are you being treated like the little fuckface prince you are, Charles? . . . But, of course, Hagerman could not imagine it, so he bounded up the flight of stairs to the third floor, where there was only Blouter's suite and the study hall. Out of breath, perspiring, gently Hagerman lifted the phone's arm from its hook, and covered the receiver with his hand.

". . . ever pull anything like that again, we're finished!"

"Oh, Charles, where is the game in you?"

"The game in me? Is that your idea of a game?"

"You don't have any game in you. You don't have any game in you at all. Not any!"

"Don't reverse things, now! I'm the one who's mad! Remember me? I had to take a taxi home!"

"Why do you have to shout so?"

"I feel like shouting! What was the big idea? Did you think it was funny?"

"I paid for the room, and if I didn't want to stay in the room, I didn't have to!"

"Who *asked* you to pay?"

"You said you didn't have any money."

"It's hopeless; talking to you about anything is hopeless."

"You're angry because I paid for the room."

"I am not angry because of that, and you know it!"

"Yes, you are. I know you are."

"Forget it! It's hopeless . . . I'll talk to you tomorrow."

"If you're going to be a grouch, don't."

"I might not!"

"You're heavy, Charles. Heavy, heavy, heavy!"

There was a click; then the sound of Shepley's voice: "Lois? Lois?"

Another click.

Hagerman hung up. Beside the telephone was a list of the Pi Pi members and pledges, with their code rings after their names. Hagerman rang his finger down the list until he came to

SHEPLEY . . . — . . .

Hagerman punched the house bell: three short rings, one long, three short.

Shepley's voice came over the intercom.

"Charles Shepley here."

"Hagerman here, Shepley. Report to the third-floor study hall."

It was after eleven; there were no lights in the study hall. Hagerman turned them on and sat down at the proctor's desk. He was not sure what he was going to say to Shepley or how he was going to manage to say it, for Hagerman was choking with rage.

On top of everything else, Shepley had used the phone room for a local call, for a call to his girl friend. Shepley, and this was the real creamer, had managed to find a girl who would pay for things.

Beautiful!

Wasn't it?

Seven

Above his head in the sky-blue room at Manhattan Holy Child Nursing Home, there hung a huge gold cross, with black enamel letters attached to it, which spelled:

LO, I
AM WITH
YOU
ALWAYS
MATTHEW 28:20

The bed was an electric one, and while his mother pressed the button that raised it to a sitting position, she said, "No one can say I don't keep you up on things, Billy. I brought *Playboy* and *Esquire* with me this morning."

The sun shone in his eyes as the bed came into position, but he did not turn his head or blink. He stayed immobile, staring straight ahead at a green and white Michigan State banner tacked to the opposite wall. He was dressed in one of the new Mod "Carnaby St." Sleepshirts, cotton, with a blue and white pattern. The nuns had shaved him at six that morning before bringing in his breakfast tray, and yesterday his hair had been shampooed with a bar of By George! shower soap.

His mother said, "I don't know what the sisters would say to my reading you such magazines," crossing to fix the blinds, so the sun would not bother his eyes, "but I've promised myself I'll see to it that you don't feel like Rip Van Winkle when you're well again."

She stared out the window at the Hudson River. Every day she looked out at the blue water and the great liners snuggled into their berths, and the George Washington Bridge glistening off in the distance, and every day she sadly remembered the Shepleys' old apartment on Riverside Drive, with a view of the river from every window, and a private elevator which opened right inside the Shepleys' foyer, and ceilings which were very high and graced with crystal chandeliers.

Where they lived now, between York and East End Avenues the view looked out on rooftops and smoking incinerators; the block was filled with teen-agers playing stickball and standing in knots listening to transistors, and men washing their cars on Sundays, and old ladies looking down on the scene from the windows above, leaning on pillows they'd dragged from their beds. The nearest park was Carl Schurz, filled with dog-do and noisy children. The East River, with its tug boats and tankers, would never be the Hudson.

She went back to the chair near the bed, and sat down, placing *Esquire* on the small table beside a glass that contained thermometers; she put *Playboy* on her lap, and wetting her fingers to make the pages move more easily, she began thumbing through it, humming a little tune from *Hello Dolly*. Her favorite line in the song was, "You're still glowing, you're still growing, you're still going strong"; she always thought of other people thinking of her, when she heard it.

Natalie Shepley was a tiny, brown-haired woman who wore turquoise-blue "owl" sunglasses with light blue prescription lenses. If she shopped at Klein's on Fourteenth Street, she always carried a large Bonwit Teller shopping bag, in which she put her purchases; before she sold any of her better apparel at thrift shops, she removed the labels to sew them into dresses, suits, and coats she had bought at Klein's or Ohrbach's or Gimbels.

She kept up on things.

She read Dorothy Manners and Suzy Knickerbocker and Craig Claiborne and Angela Taylor; she knew who Marlon Brando was dating, and who the Carter Burdens were inviting to dinner at their apartment in the Dakota, and she saved recipes for dishes like Tripe à la Mode de Caen, and she made mental notes of what Mrs. Cornelius Vanderbilt Whitney had worn to La Caravelle, and that Beatrix Wilhelmina Armgard, princess of the Netherlands and heiress presumptive to the throne, sipped Americanos at social gatherings.

She had a blond wig, and she watched "Hullabaloo" and David Susskind; she bought *Time* on Tuesdays and *Life* and *The New Yorker* on Fridays; she saw all the French and Italian movies, and she went to Wednesday matinees. She never hesitated to say that she was forty-six, for it was her conceit that she could easily pass for thirty-eight.

All the scientists at the Richmond Institute in New York City were Ph.D.'s, but she was the only wife who asked for *Dr.* Shepley when she telephoned there, and Clinton Shepley was the only one from the institute who was listed in the New York telephone directory as *Dr.*

"Remember Rip Van Winkle, Billy?" she said, as she flipped through the pages of the magazine. "When *he* woke up, the world had passed him by. That won't happen to my boy . . . Of course, thank God, *you're* not asleep . . . You know more about the world, right now, than your own father knows . . . Don't I read *everything* to you? . . . And we have such good talks . . . If you ask me, you wouldn't have enjoyed being a scientist. It's a good way to starve . . . You have too much life in you, anyway. Grandpa Shepley always said you were more like him than Clint was; do you remember him saying that? I remember your brother, I remember Charles doing imitations of Grandpa Shepley saying, 'Billy is a chip off me, and Charles is a chip off Clinton.' I think that was a fair statement."

Charles and his imitations. You never thought Charles was paying any attention to the rest of the world, and then one fine day Charles would open his mouth and John Kennedy would come out, or Frank Sinatra, or even Billy.

Natalie Shepley folded the magazine back on "The Playboy Advisor" page and paused to light a cigarette.

She said, "Billy? I'm going to read from the advice column, darling. It's a good way to keep up on things. The boys write in all sorts of questions . . . Now, here's a young man, a *D.W.* from right here in New York, and he has a very stimulating question . . . Are you ready, Billy? It seems he received an engraved calling card with the initials *P.P.C.* written on the bottom. He's writing to *Playboy* to ask what that means . . . I wouldn't have known either . . . Well, the answer is very interesting, darling, and we ought to file it for future reference. Now, bear with my French, darling. Who would ever dream I'd been to Paris, France, the way I slaughter the language! It seems that *P.P.C.* means *pour prendre congé*. That's French for 'to take one's leave,' darling. Would you have known that? It seems that the sender is either moving or will be out of town for an extended period of time. He has sent *D.W.* his card with that written on it, so *D.W.* will know—*I* wouldn't have known in a million years, and that's the truth."

Natalie Shepley sighed and took a puff on her cigarette; then she closed *Playboy* and put it on the table beside *Esquire*. She picked at her fingers a few seconds, and finally she stood up and went to the closet to get her handkerchief from the pocket of her beaver.

She said, "I'm not fooling you at all, am I, Billy? We never did succeed in keeping things from each other, did we?"

She wiped a tear from her eye and blew her nose, straightened her spectacles, and walked back to the chair by the bed. She put out her cigarette and sat down in the chair, holding her handkerchief ready in her hands. "Well," she said, "your father and I were having breakfast this morning, and the telephone rang, and your father got up from the table and answered it, and it was your brother. It was Charles. He was calling from Far Point. Well, Billy, I heard your father say, 'Oh, absolutely not, Son!' and then, 'You know better than that!' and I don't know how I knew, but I just knew that Charles had found out that I promised Pi Delta Pi that silverware . . . Remember, Billy? I read you the letter I wrote them, signing your father's name. *You* remember. We talked about it . . . I did it for his own good, darling. I did it for Charles's own good. Pi Delta Pi is *famous* for not taking legacies. Now, darling, I would have done the same thing for you, though I don't think I would have had to, because we had more money then, and those fraternities have their ways of finding out down to the last penny what the family has. . . . You were another dish of tea from Charles, too. You were fraternity material, which Charles was not, though I tried my hardest to convince him that he *was* fraternity material, so he wouldn't go through Rush Week with a complex. . . . Oh, darling, I meant well, it was—"

Natalie Shepley had to remove her glasses and wipe her eyes, blow her nose again, and muster control. "With your brother still on the phone, your father called in to me and said was I responsible for any such letter, and I said I most certainly was not responsible. Your father said was I *positive*, and I said of course I was positive, how could anyone not be positive about a thing like that, so your father told your brother, he told Charles, that someone was playing a prank on him. . . . Billy, you know I begged them in that letter to keep my offer of the silverware in strictest confidence, those were my very words, darling."

She poured herself a glass of water from the pitcher beside the thermometers, and took a few sips before she could continue. Billy gave no sign of life, save for his breathing. His eyes had the glazed look of a fish at the end of a hook. She smoothed the sheet around his waist and patted his cheek. "You'd think a national fraternity would respect a confidential matter," she said, "but the long and the short of it is that someone told Charles, and when your father was finished reassuring Charles that he had written no such letter, that I hadn't either, he came back into the dining room, and he said, 'Natalie, why in the name of God didn't you let the boy go on his own steam?' . . . I could never fool Clint, either . . . Darling, I just sat there and had a cry. I'm in tears right now, too, Billy. I don't know if you can tell that or not, but my eyes are filled with tears right now . . . Then your father said, 'The Pi Pi who told him is trying to take it back now, but I doubt that we've heard the end of the matter, Natalie. I think this is only the beginning of a very unhappy experience for Charles.'

"Billy, I told your father that we should pray that it *is* the end of the matter, that we should never admit that we wrote any such letter, and, darling, your father was not very nice to me at all, not at all nice. '*We* didn't write the letter!' he shouted at me. '*You* wrote the letter.' I said that I wrote it for Charles's own good, and that I did not think very highly of a fraternal organization which would break a trust, and your father said, no, I wrote it for my own good. Which just," sobbing, forcing herself to go on, "just doesn't," pausing, handkerchief at her nose, "make sss-ssen-sense."

Then Natalie Shepley let the tears flow out of her eyes and roll down her cheeks onto the Thermo-weave covering Billy, and she put her arms around her son and hugged him to her.

"Oh, Billy, what is Easter going to be like now?"

William Shepley had no answer to that one, either.

But Easter was going to be fine as far as Charles Shepley

was concerned. He whistled while he walked through campus town that warm March morning on the day of The Divine Comedy. He bought a cup of coffee at the Unmuzzled Ox, and did not even cruise the coat racks or look for tips left on empty tables. Nor would he have to sell his stereophonic phonograph when he went home for Easter. He had a far more lucrative source of income now. He had Hagerman right in his hip pocket, on tape.

After Hagerman had blown his top in the study hall last night, he had come down to Shepley's room and told Thorpe to get out. His hands had shook, and he had wet-lipped the stinky cigarette he was smoking, and while he was talking to Shepley, pacing back and forth like a rat caught in a maze, Charles had reached down under the bed and snapped Thorpe's Webcor over to *Record*.

—Shepley, we can straighten this thing out right now.
—How?
—Not by going to Blouter, Shepley.
—That's where I'm going, when Blouter gets back.
—It was a gag, Shepley.
—Ha! Ha!
—A gag.
—Har de har, har, har . . . If my father promised this fraternity silverware to pledge me, this fraternity had better go shopping for silverware, because the gift has just been rescinded.
—Shepley, Shep—look, I said that it was just a gag.
—I'm still going to ask Blouter.
—Shep, listen to me. I don't want you to MENTION THIS TO BLOUTER!
—What's the difference, if it's just a gag? Mike could use a good laugh, couldn't he?
—Shepley, Shep—can't you take a little kidding?
—You weren't kidding, Hagerman. You were lying, but you weren't kidding.
—I said I was lying. I said that, Shep.
—So what's the difference?
—Blouter doesn't want the pledges running to him over every little thing. What do you think Blouter's going to think of you?
—I don't care. . . . It doesn't sound so little, either.
—It's LITTLE, Shepley! A little joke, was all. Are you going to make an ass of yourself in front of Blouter? Can't you take a little joke?

—Is it big enough to get me out of The Divine Comedy, Hagerman?

—To *what?*

—You heard me, Hagerman. I want out.

—You want me to make an exception of you, is that it?

—That's it.

—Always the exception, huh, Shepley? Always looking for an out.

—*Always,* Hagerman. . . . What about it?

—I don't believe that you actually mean that. What kind of a man are you?

—Yes or no, Hagerman.

—Is that what you really want?

—Shall I put it in writing for you?

—You won't go to Blouter?

—No.

—Did you tell Thorpe about this?

—No.

—You didn't tell anyone?

—Not a soul.

—Okay, Shepley. Okay.

Then Hagerman had left, after arranging for Shepley to bluff participation in The Divine Comedy, and Shepley had slipped the tape off the recorder, substituted another for it from Thorpe's drawer, and put the tape in the pocket of his tweed jacket.

"What's with Hagerman tonight?" Thorpe had asked, when he returned to the room.

"We've got separate itineraries now. We won't be going together tomorrow, Dan."

"Shep, he's got it in for you."

"Yeah."

"I just saw his face when he came out of here, Shep."

"Uh-huh."

"You're pretty cool. Have you forgotten Osmond?"

"Not at all."

Shepley had insomnia most of the night, falling asleep only toward dawn, then jerking awake to remember his plan. First, to go to campus town, where he would call home and verify what he already knew: that Hagerman *had* been lying. Then, to stop in at the Co-op Book and Record Store, to see if the tape had taken. . . . Next on the agenda was the confrontation with Hagerman. For it had not been long last night until Charles Shepley realized that anything important enough for Hagerman to cancel an Inferno itinerary over also had a price, particularly when it was on record.

So Charles Shepley left the Unmuzzled Ox and set off for the Pi Delta Pi house, with the morning sun and this colossal piece of luck to warm him, ready to haggle with Hagerman.

Hagerman had not slept well either, despite a Compazine, a Librium, and two Doridens. His bedside table looked like the Valley of the Dolls. When he had managed to convince himself that he had nothing to worry about, that it was obvious Shepley believed he had invented the silverware story, and would be satisfied to drop the whole thing if he could get out of The Divine Comedy, Hagerman had drifted into sleep only to be blasted awake by Burroughs' snoring. Then all the anxieties returned; then the sands of his security shifted back and he was adrift again, with palpitations and his insides twanging, and all the horrid remembrances of Len the Man and Peg Beauty parading across the screen of his mind, and the incubus of Blouter holding the power to deactivate Hagerman, and Shepley with the ammunition to trigger it.

He could just hear Peg Beauty:

"Peter, what did you do *this* time?"

And Len the Man:

"He didn't do anything in particular. It's never anything, in particular; it's everything in general, starting with the fact he's little and ugly and doesn't know Number two has to try harder."

Actually.

Len the Man had actually come out with that one when Peter had been sent home from Sunstone Military Academy.

Oh, he was smiling; you don't use the toothpaste for people who can't brush after every meal and *not* smile; you're *always* on if you're Len Lovely; if you have a headache, you don't take it out on the kid, even if the kid is the reason you have the headache. Goldfinger smiles in the face of all obstacles and pushes on.

Hagerman had finally carried his pillow down to the Pi Pi living room. He had sat on the couch smoking cigarettes and waiting for his stomach to stop dancing, and he had picked up a copy of yesterday's *Far Point Record* to take his mind off all of it. On the front page there was a picture of a Mrs. Matilda Holt from Valley Stream Road in Far Point;

she was sitting in a chair with antimacassars on the arms, leaning into a GE radio with a dazed smile on her face, holding in her lap a huge photograph of a soldier with lieutenant's bars on his shirt.

MRS. MATILDA HOLT HOLDS A PICTURE OF HER SON, MARINE LT. JOSEPH HOLT, WHILE LISTENING TO RADIO IN HER FAR POINT HOME. INTERVIEW WITH JOSEPH BY WABC RADIO WAS BEAMED HERE YESTERDAY. A WIDOW, MRS. HOLT LIVES FOR SON'S RETURN.

"We always underestimated Joey," she said. "You know how it is sometimes with kids. They don't seem to be going anywhere."

Joseph Holt was going somewhere last Saturday. He was going across a river in the Mekong Delta 115 miles southwest of Saigon. He was going into Cong country.

"The other kids used to call him 'Turtle,'" Mrs. Holt recalled, "because Joey was always sticking his neck out, but we called it getting into trouble, because that's what it always came down to in the end."

Joseph Holt was sticking his neck out again; he was getting into trouble again. Plenty of trouble. The kind of trouble that could easily kill him.

"Joey's father and me didn't know what a brave boy we had."

Six Cong guerillas soon knew what a brave boy Joey Holt was; it was the last lesson they were ever taught. Joey taught it to them with an M14 rifle, and plenty of good old American guts!

"When Joey comes home, he'll be king in this house."

He's king to the Cong right now. He's the reason they don't sleep so well these days. Joey Holt is the reason we sleep better, knowing he's—

Hagerman had slapped the newspaper to the floor and ground out his cigarette. He had curled up on the couch and put the pillow in against his stomach where it ached, and then he had taken deep breaths, which sometimes helped his attacks of anxiety, and in a little while he felt the tension start to taper off. . . . Shepley believed him; Shepley was not going to make an ass of himself by going to Blouter. He had let things grow way out of proportion again, was all; weeping Jesus, Hagerman, don't let every little thing grab you this way; steady, Hagerman; slow down, buster;

soothing himself as he had often done when he was a kid, holding himself and whispering softly to himself in the dark, until he was fast sleep.

Then his 'copter was disabled by ground fire, and he crash-landed in Victor Charlie territory, and in the night a white phosphorus mortar shell exploded, and the valley erupted in recoilless cannon and machine-gun fire and the flash of shells. He stuck it out, the green beret cocked jauntily over one eye; he braved the hail of fire to rescue the 'copter's pilot; he sprinted past a spray of bullets, while choppers and planes went after him. And when he woke up with the sun in his eyes, dive bombers were coming to the aid of the besieged band of men he led; he was safe and sure, and rubbing his eyes, Hagerman smiled.

The feeling the dream gave him lingered.

It was a warm, bright morning, a perfect morning for The Divine Comedy.

He showered and shaved and polished his loafers, was Mother Varner's escort for breakfast, was high-spirited at the chapter meeting where he assigned actives to guide pledges on their Infernos, was snapping his fingers and singing up in his room, when Shepley appeared.

"Can we have a little private talk, Hagerman?"

"Now what do you want to get out of, Shepley?"

Shepley had smiled then, and then Shepley had given it to him: the shaft.

"Out of debt, Hagerman."

Eight

Lois Faye had a dream.

It was to have her own apartment on East Fifty-seventh Street in New York.

It was to have an answering service and a garage for the car.

It was to have a Yorkie she would probably call Canapé and a canary she would probably call Peter Duchin.

Last summer Lois Faye had spent a week visiting Terry Swan. "Swanny" and Lois had gone to Briar Hall together; Swanny had graduated a year ahead of Lois, flunked out of a junior college in Vermont, and talked her parents into letting her take an apartment between Third and Lexington on East Fifty-seventh. She was supposed to be studying Speedwriting; she was supposed to be looking for a job in publishing. She subscribed to Telanserphone and kept her Mustang in the garage of the apartment house. She had a Yorkie named Truffle and a canary named Lester Lanin.

"I can remember when we had to go into a closet to smoke," Lois had told her, "and now look at you! You have everything!"

"Oh, yes," she told Lois in a Martin Luther King accent; "we on de move!"

And Lois Faye had burst out laughing, because that was her kind of humor; she didn't have anything against Martin Luther King, but all of that was something else; she felt relieved when she was with someone like Swanny; Swanny's place was just the kind of place Lois Faye would fix up—not a cutesy apartment with modern chairs that looked like dogs begging, and gimcracks from Serendipity and Greenbranch, no gum machines or Tiffany lamps, no café curtains, no travel posters or Toulouse-Lautrec Jane Avril reproductions, no unpainted furniture from Macy's stained walnut, not any of that jazz, but a serious-looking scene: a Queen Anne settee, a Stiffel table lamp finished in old antique brass, a tambour desk from the Baker collection, a silver bonbon dish from Gorham; elegant, restrained, the sort of place a stockbroker would be comfortable in.

Swanny had not made a home for herself; she had fixed up a trap for the likes of Credit Card Carl, Wally Wallet, Chase Manhattan Marvin, and Bankers Trust Blum.

"For myself, I'd like all white," she had told Lois; "white rugs, white furniture, I'd wear all white—I love white—but white is too hooker. The hookers ruined white and poodles. You have to look as though you wander into Parke-Bernet to browse at auctions; you have to look as though you usually go to the openings at Wildenstein. You don't wear wool after five and you don't wear mink in the daytime. White is out. Unless you want to marry some guy who wears green suits and owns a handkerchief factory."

Listening to Swanny talk was like having a vision or hearing a prophet; it was the Word. It said it all. Lois Faye burned for more; she burned to go and live in New York. She crammed her handbag with matchbooks (which Swanny kept in a Steuben bowl) from the Plaza, the Ground Floor, the Forum of the Twelve Caesars, the Top of the Six's, and she went back to South Orange, New Jersey, and moped around and complained about having to attend F.P.C.

Her mother said, "I never had an education. You're going to."

"What for? I want to get married someday."

"All the more reason. Who's going to marry you in New York?"

"There are lots of men there. Men, not boys. Men with money."

"Your father doesn't want you to marry a millionaire. He wants you to marry someone with something up here," tapping her head.

"What about what I want?"

"You got your mink, didn't you? You got your Thunderbird, didn't you? Think of your father, for a change. Try
college. Will it kill you to try?"

"I'll be a dud-avocado. I'm a half-breed. You fixed me up
good, marrying a Jew."

"Do I hold it against you that you're a Jew? Don't hold
it against me that I married one."

"Very funny."

"Try college. Rich boys get educated, too."

"Not at Far Point College."

"You wouldn't know one if you fell over one. They're
very subtle."

Take Charles Shepley, for example; take the afternoon of
the Inferno.

"Charles?"

"What?"

"Are you rich?"

"Sure."

"Is that why you don't have to be in the Inferno?"

"Not exactly."

"Yes, it is."

"No, not really."

"Yes it is. I know it is."

"All right. It is."

"You're rich and that's why you don't want things."

"Umm-hmmm."

"And you don't propose, for you are trifling with me."

"Propose? I have three more years of college."

"But you don't have to be anything, because you're rich,
so you don't have to be graduated."

"You have it all figured out . . . Watch for a red barn on
the left."

"Don't order me around or I'll get on my high horse!"

"Look. You want to go into New York, don't you? You
want to buy the Pucci, don't you, and see your friend
Swanny, and go to the Plaza, don't you?"

"Yes."

"Then watch for a red barn on the left."

"I *hate* this sort of thing!"

"Do you think I like it?"

"What'd we have to pack a hamper of sandwiches for?
What do we have to act like we're going on a picnic for?"

"*You* didn't have to pack anything."

"It's in my *car!*"

"So there's a hamper of sandwiches in your car; is that too much to ask of you?"

"It's going to smell up this car."

"We'll throw them out, Lois, as soon as I've made the rendezvous with Hagerman."

"The *rendezvous*. It sounds like bad James Bond."

"Okay, okay. Just do what I tell you, and it'll all be over very fast."

"It's for kids."

"Most fraternity stuff is!"

"Did you have to join a fraternity to please your father who is a tycoon in his own right?"

"You guessed it."

"You don't even smile. You *are* heavy!"

"There it is! Stay to your left."

"Ho hum."

"It isn't my idea of an afternoon's fun, either."

"What if Hagerman makes you stay here for hours?"

"He won't. I just had to look like I was setting off on an Inferno."

"The stores close at six."

"I know when the stores close. I *live* in New York, remember?"

"I'm just a taxi!"

"I'm sorry about it . . . Now turn off here."

"I don't know why *I* had to come along on this secret rendezvous. Why couldn't you have met me after?"

"Because I didn't want to take a bus out here and back."

"Why can't I meet this Hagerman?"

"Because you can't. I don't want him to know anyone's around."

"Is he rich, too?"

"We're all millionaires. Okay?"

"What if he sees my car?"

"That's why we're here early, so he won't see the car."

"I may just call out to him, 'Hagerman, come and see the car!' "

"Do that. And kiss your Pucci goodbye."

"I like a fun millionaire. You're not a fun millionaire."

"When this is over, I'll be lots of fun."

"Where will we go for dinner?"

"Longchamps. Okay?"

It would not surprise her if he were serious. On his own,

Charles Shepley never suggested anything expensive to do. She forgave him the Bluebird of Happiness, because it was the only place near Far Point where students could go for that, but when they went to dinner, he never picked the Villa Arturo in Dobbs Ferry, or the Water Wheel Inn in Ardsley, or Le Gai Pinguin in White Plains; *she* had to suggest places like that, or they would wind up in some awful four-dollar student steak house.

He was never reluctant to go to the better places; it was just that, left to his own devices, he would not take her to them.

He was a little *too* subtle for Lois Faye.

Her mother was right, she would not have known Charles Shepley was rich if she had fallen over him.

Little things gave him away. He was certainly not in the millionaire class, Lois Faye didn't *think*, but he had money. Her first inkling had come when he had actually ordered a bottle of champagne for them on the night she had met him. She was always telling boys she wanted champagne. Usually they asked the waiter for a couple of highballs; at best, a champagne cocktail, but Charles had ordered a full bottle without batting an eye. He had been to Europe with his family; he lived in the 500 block in the East Eighties, which meant East End Avenue, veddy chic; he paid for the room at the Bluebird, whether or not they used it; he could blow thirty dollars on dinner without so much as a frown when the waiter brought the check. . . . On the subject of money, Charles Shepley was a very cool character. And he gambled.

But he was a boy. Just as he did not whisk her off for continental cuisine in an elegant setting without a little prodding, neither did he surprise her with a string of real pearls, or a little gold bracelet; he needed a push, a diagram. He did not know how to do, and it was probably because he didn't that Lois Faye found herself not the least intimidated by him, and consequently not in any way inhibited with him.

"What *is* it with you and me?" she would ask him sometimes in bed.

"What's what?"

"Why doesn't it *hurt?* It's supposed to hurt a girl."

"Not if she wants it."

"What do I *want* it for?"

"Why don't you just enjoy it?"

"I *do* . . . I hate it!"

"You're probably in love with me."

"No, I'm not!"

"We're probably in love."

"We are *not!*"

"Then what is it with you and me?"

"I don't know. I hate it!"

She did hate it, too, because sometimes she could not stop herself.

"It's chemistry," Terry Swan had told her flatly, over a drink at the Drake, during Christmas vacation. "It's not a good thing to happen the first time, darling."

"Why?"

"You'll imagine you're in love with him."

"Hunh-uh. He's not my dish. Very unsophisticated."

"Wait until you kiss Sidney Sophisticated. You'll go scampering back to dear old Charlie. Chemistry is lethal. I'm glad it didn't happen to me the first time. I'd be a dancing teacher's wife. My chemistry lesson teaches the merengue to over-forties."

"You didn't marry *him?*"

"I might've, if I'd been your age when I met him."

"Anyway, Charles never mentions marriage; we're very cool."

"What are you going to say if he asks you?"

"I'm going to tell him that I want to come to New York, that I don't feel like settling down so soon."

"If you've gotten that far in your fantasies, you want him to ask you."

"No I don't!"

"Sure you do, darling!"

"I do not. Not at all!"

But it did bother her that Charles Shepley took her for granted. No one ever really jokes; last night's little trick of running out on him while he was in the bathroom at the Bluebird had made her laugh, but her sense of humor had not given her the sudden impulse to flee. Nor had it been all that easy to leave, after the session on the bed beforehand, nor had she rested very well back in bed at the dorm.

He had his hold on her; it had nothing to do with a Pucci blouse, but Charles Shepley was not going to know it.

She parked her car where he told her to, a half mile down from the red barn on the road to Pearl River, about fifteen miles from Far Point.

"Why can't I come with you? I'll hide behind the barn."

"Lois, will you just do this one little thing the way I want it done?"

"What'll you buy me?"

"The Pucci; *right?*"

"That's for coming out here," she laughed, "not for sitting in the car while you go off on a mysterious rendezvous." ·

He said, "Just be good. You owe it to me after last night."

"I paid for the room."

"Why don't you just sit here in the car and make up a sign with 'I Paid For The Room' written on it? Okay?"

"I may not be here when you come back."

"That wouldn't surprise me, either."

He got the hamper out of the back of the car, and trudged down the road with it, and Lois Faye snapped on the radio and lit a cigarette. She was on her sixth cigarette when she saw a red Corvair pull up to the barn in the distance.

The whole sorority-fraternity thing was too much.

Last night out in front of the Unmuzzled Ox, she had come upon a group of girls on their knees making Praise Allah gestures and singing: "I am so goddam glad that I am ma Ka-ap-pa, Ka-ap-pa, Ka-ap-pa, Gam-am-ah"; a tall red-headed girl standing over them while they sang had waited until they finished, and then commanded them to flush like toilets. They had all flattened out on their bellies in their heels and hose and pushed their bottoms up and down and made gurgling sounds, while a crowd gathered to laugh.

Try college.

I never had an education; you're going to.

So for a while she kept on listening to the radio, and then she smoked her seventh cigarette, and then she got out of the car and stretched.

Secret rendezvous.

Hah!

She started walking toward the red barn in her yellow poor boy and her purple bell-bottoms and her white round-toed boots, giggling to think of Charles looking up in the midst of his rendezvous and seeing her off in the adjoining cornfield posed as a scarecrow.

But when she was halfway there, the Corvair zoomed away from the barn, kicking up a dust cloud behind it.

She found Charles on his knees near the barn door, picking up pieces of silverware which had fallen from the hamper.

"What happened?"

"Hagerman had a little temper fit. He kicked the hamper over."

"Did you pay him off?"

"Yeah, yeah. It's all settled; as soon as I get this stuff picked up, we'll take off."

"I have to change my clothes."

"Why can't you go like you are? I'm not supposed to be seen in Far Point until the Inferno's over."

"Will you be embarrassed if I'm like this?"

"No . . . pick up that thermos, will you?"

"Where'd *it* come from?"

"It belongs to the house. Hagerman brought it with him."

"Why? What's in it?"

"Ice. He was going to have a drink with me. Then he changed his mind."

"I *love* a mystery."

"So do I. He came out here in a good mood, and left in his usual foul temper."

"What'd you do?"

"Nothing he didn't count on . . . I pity Dan Thorpe."

"I don't pity any of you. You're all silly!"

"Dan's got to go on his Inferno with Hagerman."

"I am bored, bored, bored . . . I didn't stay in the car."

"I see you didn't."

"I won't do *anything* you say."

"Hand me the thermos. Let's get going."

"I'm going to keep the thermos," she said.

"Okay, keep it."

"Charles? Would I be less pushy if I weren't half-Jewish and the Kappa Kappa Gammas had asked me to pledge?"

"I like you the way you are," he answered. "Nuts."

Nine

The highway between Pearl River and Far Point was peppered with drab roadhouses which smelled of draught beer and chloride of lime, and kept the jukebox and television going at the same time. One of them was Eddie's, where Thorpe had been ordered to meet Hagerman at three that afternoon. It was five thirty now. *Beyond Mombasa* was going into the stretch over the bar, while Donna Reed's words were almost lost to the noise of "Spanish Flea" by the Tijuana Brass. Thorpe and Hagerman were on a chit for five Hanky Bannisters apiece, and Thorpe's mood had swung from fear of Hagerman to envy of the other Pi Pi pledges, who were rumored to be down at Aunt Sate's house near the Far Point bag factory.

Thorpe's Inferno was a real fizzle; it had turned into Batman and Robin, with Batman issuing long maudlin soliloquies about the burdens of his office, and Robin wondering if Shepley was tied to the New York Central tracks over in Tarrytown, or set adrift off the Far Point Boat Basin in Far Point.

At first, Hagerman's conciliatory disposition had come as a welcome miracle; then it had begun to pall, as Thorpe's ears grew tired of Cornel Wilde and Donna Reed competing with Cher and Petula Clark and Herman's Hermits and The Supremes, and his buttocks ached from the hard wooden chair; now, Thorpe was bored and a little high, and growing more outspoken in his responses to Hagerman.

When Hagerman signaled the waiter for another round, Thorpe let go an exasperated sigh that penetrated even Hagerman's self-involvement.

"What's that for, Dan?"

"I'm getting smashed, aren't you?"

"One more. Then we have to think about your Inferno."

"I wouldn't mind a crack at Aunt Sate's girls."

"I don't take my pledges where the other actives take theirs."

"Where's Shepley?"

"Dan, don't take liberties."

"I just wondered."

"I'm sorry you have to room with someone like Charles Shepley."

"Shep's okay."

"He's a very dangerous boy, very goddam sick."

"Shep?"

"Shep. He's like all of them. Osmond and Blouter and even Burroughs."

"I don't get you, Peter."

"You know how they are about their families. When a man pledges a fraternity, he should leave all that behind him."

"All what?"

"All that going home and writing home and calling home. You know, Dan, we're never heroes in their eyes; that's crap, Dan! You know, Dan, a man will stick his neck out and his folks will call it getting into trouble."

"Huh?"

"That's the truth. They don't know how brave their sons are. Then they try to take all the credit. *After* a man's been through hell!"

The waiter brought them two more and Thorpe said, "We ought to take the check now, don't you think, Peter?"

"The check will be there when we're ready."

"I don't think I'm following what you're saying."

"The check isn't going to blow away, Dan."

"I mean about a man going through hell and his folks taking all the credit."

"You're not listening."

"Yes, I am."

"You're not paying attention."

"I am, Peter."

"You know, we have a very weak chapter here at Far Point. The pledges think they can go over the actives' heads."

"I *didn't* know that."

"You remember what Osmond pulled?"

"Well. His mother died."

"I didn't kill his mother."

"I guess that was an exception."

"An exception? No. Standard procedure for the kind of mother-lovers we pledge. Run to Blouter. Cry on Blouter's shoulder. When Blouter's not home crying on his mother's shoulder . . . Dan, I'll tell you something: Shepley better get off my back."

"What does that mean?"

"You tell him that."

"Okay."

"You tell him I'm not going to put up with his threats."

"Shep *threatened* you?"

"He's dangerous, Dan. There's something wrong with his mind."

"What'd he threaten you about?"

"He just threatened me, that's all."

"What did you do to him?"

"Dan, I am exactly five foot one and one-half inches tall. Charles Shepley is five foot ten, at least. What could I do to him?"

"I don't know, but I can't imagine Shep threatening anyone."

"That's what they always say about killers, isn't it? He was such a nice boy. Such a good boy. So attentive to his mommy and daddy."

"Oh, wow!"

"What?"

"I don't know what the hell we're talking about."

"Do you know the words to 'I'll Feel Blessed'?"

"Yes."

"Sing them."

"Here?"

"Here. Now."

Thorpe sang very softly:

> If the Chinese drop the bomb
> Or I'm sent to Vietnam,
> I'll still—

Then Hagerman joined in, singing at the top of his lungs:

> I'll still feel blessed.
> If a Pi Pi pin is on my chest,
> I'll still feel blessed.
> If I have to die—

Thorpe could feel his face turn red as the men at the bar turned to stare. Hagerman was waving his swizzle stick above his head; he was wearing a blue and white Pi Delta Pi blazer, and his diamond pin was pinned onto his shirt over his heart.

> Let my last words be Pi Pi.
> When the discotheques are dead,
> When we've licked the last damn Red,
> I'll still feel blessed.
> If a Pi Pi pin is on my chest,
> I'll still feel blessed.

Thorpe pretended he had to use the men's in a hurry.

When he came out, Hagerman was not at the table. The check was there with money on top of it; Thorpe looked around and saw Hagerman up near the phone booth with the Far Point directory spread before him; he was running his finger down the column of a page.

When he walked back to the table, he said: "Lasciate ogni speranza, voi ch'entrate."

"Conosco i segni dell' antica fiamma," Thorpe managed; he had practiced the response all morning.

"Let's go," said Hagerman.

He reached up and fastened a button to the lapel of Thorpe's sport coat. It said: "Mothers, let the Vietnamese do it themselves!"

Thorpe laughed. "Where'd you get that?"

"They're on sale at the Co-op."

Then Hagerman began bellowing, "Pi Pi, my love for you is why I strive," and again Thorpe blushed while the customers in Eddie's gave them drop-dead looks, but as he left there arm-in-arm with Hagerman, he figured what the hell, Hagerman wasn't such a bad guy after all, just a little bombed, same as Thorpe.

They sang all the way into Far Point; Thorpe even sang

"China" to "Dinah," and Hagerman actually joined in: "China, is there any place wiser? Won't we ever recognize her—" and when Hagerman's Corvair pulled up in front of a small white bungalow on a quiet street in the residential section of Far Point, they were weak from laughing, and really feeling the Hanky Bannister. It was dark now; the streetlights were on, and over the car radio Edward P. Morgan was beginning his evening commentary.

Hagerman offered Thorpe one of his French cigarettes.

"I don't smoke."

"That's right. You take pretty good care of the old body, don't you, Dan?"

"I guess I do."

"That's why I wouldn't take you down to Aunt Sate's place."

"I wouldn't have minded."

"You could get the syph from one of her girls, Dan. I take better care of you than that."

"Thanks, Peter. . . . Where are we?"

"We're at Matilda's, Dan. She might not be much to look at, but don't let that fool you. Matilda's the best lay this side of the river."

Thorpe looked at the small white bungalow. It had a picture window and there was a light on in the living room, and Thorpe could see a ledge near the window with plants resting on it.

Hagerman said, "She works by herself."

"Here?"

"Looks just like an ordinary home, doesn't it?"

"Yeah."

"Well, it's a cat house, boy, and there's a pussycat inside waiting for some action. Matilda. Five bucks for fifteen minutes."

"Geez, Peter, I don't know. I had a lot to drink."

"You're in shape, Dan. Go ahead."

"What'll I say? Geez, Peter, do I just walk up and ring the bell?"

"Just walk up and ring the bell. Tell her you want to talk to her in private. Tell her 'Turtle' sent you. When you get inside, tell her Turtle said she'd give you fifteen minutes for five dollars."

"I *have* to do it, huh?"

"Dan, I'm doing you a favor. You don't want to get the

syph from one of Aunt Sate's girl! Now, get going, pledge! Hop to it, mother-lover!"

Thorpe sighed.

"Do you have five?" Hagerman asked.

"Yes."

"She'll look like anything but what she is, Thorpe, but don't let that throw you off."

Thorpe pushed down on the door handle.

Hagerman said, "I'll be waiting, pledge."

"Yeah," Thorpe said. "Okay."

He went up the walk with some difficulty; the Scotch had finally reached his legs. At the door, he took a deep breath, let it out, straightened himself up, and gave the bell an aggressive punch. He had been with a whore before, but there had been others with him, and they had gone to a real house with a dozen or more girls in it, and it had been late at night, down on the Jersey shore, in the middle of summer.

He punched the bell again.

Then a woman opened the door; she had black hair with streaks of gray in it, and harlequin glasses, and she was wearing an apron over her dress. She was old enough to be Thorpe's mother.

"Yes?"

"May I come in?"

"What do you want?"

She was drying her hands on her apron; Thorpe could smell hamburger cooking.

He said, "Turtle sent me."

"He *did?*"

She smiled and stepped back, and Thorpe walked into a foyer filled with wall racks containing more plants. He could see Chet Huntley on the television in the living room, and he stood there uncertainly while she shut the door and led him inside.

"He's all right, isn't he?"

"Sure. Yes."

There were antimacassars on the arms and backs of all the chairs and the couch, and there was a bag with knitting spilling out of it on a glass-top coffee table.

She said, "Sit down."

He did, in a slat-back chair, and she sat on the couch.

"I was just getting dinner," she said.

He felt suddenly very drunk. He said, "I can smell it."

"Are you hungry?"

"No. I've been drinking."

"Where do you know Joey from?"

"Who?"

"We never liked the name Turtle," she smiled.

"He gave me a message."

"Would you like some coffee? I don't keep liquor."

"Look, let's get it over with. Turtle said you'd go fifteen minutes for five dollars."

"I beg your pardon?"

"Look, Matilda, it's all right. I'm from the college."

"What are you talking about?"

"Don't you want to make five dollars?"

"How?"

Thorpe laughed. He giggled. She was like somebody's goddam mother.

She said, "Maybe you'd better come back when you're sober, Mr.—Mr.—what *is* your name?"

"I'm sober enough, Matilda. Why don't we just go into the bedroom?"

"What?"

She was on her feet now, edging over toward the fireplace. She actually looked as though she were afraid of Thorpe.

Thorpe said, "I'm from the college, Matilda."

"Get out of here!" She was reaching for an andiron.

"Wait a minute!" Thorpe stood up, lurched against the coffee table, and stood swaying. "Wait a minute! Turtle sent me. Do you want to make five dollars or not? You don't have to hit me over the head. Just tell me yes or no."

"No! Get out of here!"

"Okay, okay! What are you in business for?"

"Get out of my house!"

"I'm going. What the hell is the matter with you?"

"You scum! Get out of my house!" and she was starting for him with the andiron.

On his way down the walk, running, he fell on one knee. Hagerman called to him, "Get up! Hurry!"

He reached the car, and Hagerman took off before he had the door closed.

The wheels squeaked as they rounded the corner.

"Was she really a whore, Hagerman?"

"What'd she say?"

"She told me to get out of her house."

"Maybe it was the wrong place."

"No. She knew who Turtle was, all right."

"Maybe she just wasn't in the mood, Dan."
"She sure wasn't!"
"Well, Matilda's moody, Dan."
"I'm pretty smashed, Peter."
"Your Inferno's over, pledge."
"Wasn't much of an Inferno," Thorpe mumbled.
Hagerman laughed. "It was for Matilda."

Ten

Charles Shepley was not prepared for Terry Swan.

What he had expected was a Rona Jaffe *Best of Everything* type, who was very chic, but had stockings drying in the tub behind the shower curtain, and was just a little shy with Charles in the beginning, though they would become fast buddies before the night was over, exchanging whatta-nut-Lois-is stories; he would no doubt even break down and ask her to join them for dinner. He had gotten $150 from Hagerman for the tape; he had paid forty-some for the Pucci, and he needed enough to get through the Rabbit Hop, but he could still afford dinner for three, if they went somewhere up in the East Eighties like Bell's or Beggi's or Dorian's.

What she had on was hipster pants of checked white flannel, with a red, white, and blue flag blouse that came just below her breasts, leaving several inches of bare skin between the pants and top; bare arms, save for a huge square wristwatch with a white leather strap, and shiny silver boots. Her black hair was cut like Rudolph Nureyev's, to whom she bore a faint resemblance; her long, dangling, black-and-white papier-mâché pinwheel earrings hung down past her shoulders.

When Charles and Lois walked into her apartment, she was standing there with an English Oval hanging from her lips, spraying herself with a newly opened two-ounce size of Celui.

When Charles said, "Ummm. Celui," she said, "The boy can read; that's what college does for you."

"This is Charles Shepley, Terry."

"Hi, Charles."

"Hi . . . Celui is the only perfume I *can* recognize. Lois wears it."

"I do *not!*" from Lois.

"C-e-l-u-i?" Charles spelled it out.

"Of course I don't!"

"I thought—" he stopped when he felt her fingernails digging into the back of his hands.

Terry Swan sprayed some of the perfume at Lois. "I know you copy me, darling," she said. "Don't be humiliated."

But Lois Faye's face was a brilliant red and Charles knew that right at that moment she loathed him.

A stereophonic hidden from view was playing Miss D.'s "Perdido," and now the whole room reeked of the perfume, and Terry Swan was gliding around snapping her fingers and singing, "Perdido, I looked for my heart; it's perdido; I lost it way down in Toredo—" and asking, "What'll you have to drink?"

They told her and she still danced around, into the kitchen for the ice bucket and glasses—"Bolero, I glanced as we danced the Bolero"—out to the cabinet where she kept her liquor—"Bolero, I glanced as we danced the Bolero"—and finally all three were fixed with drinks and settled in a semicircle.

"You chose the perfect day to come in," she said. "There's a crowd coming by and we're all going to the Cheetah."

"Can I go like this?"

"Sure, anything goes. Oh my God, you should have seen the South American I met there two weeks ago. Rich as Croesus. He took me to the Kaleidoscope and spent three hundred and fifty dollars on me in about ten minutes. Like that." She snapped her fingers for emphasis.

Lois said, "I just got the most divine Pucci blouse."

"Ugh and *ugh!* I hate anything but the pants. Darling, go to the Kaleidoscope or Splendiferous or Paraphernalia. Puccis are dullsville. Buy something ghastly, or you'll feel like last year, darling. I might even break down and get a big Heinz pickle for over my fireplace, and you know how I try to keep my castle conservative."

Charles said, "It's a very nice apartment."

She looked at him as though he were a tradesman and for

some unbeknown reason had taken it into his head to sit down in her living room; then she continued to direct her conversation to Lois. Lois's few glances in his direction were no more approving; he knew he would never hear the end of the Celui thing.

"Anyway," said Terry Swan, "this South American is separated from his wife; they're all Catholics down there so they never get divorced, but he lives all alone in this huge manse and he's panting for me to come down and go skinny dipping with him every night in this big swimming pool he's got shaped like a banana; he sent me a picture of it. I said send me the ticket, round-trip, and I'd get around to it sooner or later, and I opened my mail the other day and damn near fainted right in front of the doorman, because there was the ticket, round-trip; he couldn't have left New York any longer than twenty-six hours. So I marched myself down to Pan Am this morning and *voilà*. I'm going to buy some A.T. and T. with some of the money; it's way down now."

Lois was laughing now, and managing to say, "You cashed it in? Oh, Swanny," chortle, huff, hee-haw, gasp, "really! Have you no *shame?*"

"The thing that makes me really sick-in-bed is that I didn't tell him I couldn't come without a girl friend for a chaperone, because he would have fallen for that; I could have gotten twice as much."

"I love it!" said Lois Faye.

Charles Shepley looked at her and realized he had rarely seen her as happy, as comfortable, as at home, anywhere.

He got up eventually and fixed himself a drink, since neither of the girls gave any indication they were going to offer to do that; they hardly paid attention as he dropped the ice into his glass, went into the kitchen for water, and set his drink on the counter there, and then began a search for the bathroom.

There were papers down on the floor for the Yorkshire and the Yorkshire was sitting inside a straw house under the sink, with a red velvet ribbon in her hair. She was chewing on one end of a rubber toy shaped like a hot dog in a roll, complete with a glob of yellow mustard on top. Charles leaned down and played with her for awhile; he urinated and washed his hands, waited for them to dry by themselves rather than soil the flimsy light-blue hand towels on the brass rack, and made a solemn face in the mirror, a smiling one, an angry one, and one of Dr. Jekyll turning into Mr. Hyde. Then he flushed the toilet and put down the seat, and looked at his watch. It was five thirty.

He had not liked the idea of going to the Plaza for drinks, because the drinks there were very expensive, but he had looked forward to taking Lois there, because he had imagined it would be a huge treat for her, and he would have liked to see her face while they sat there and looked at one another— she was very good at that, looking at someone across the table with a very intense expression. It was all turning out rather badly. He had hoped she would savor some of the things, like buying the Pucci—he had hoped she would bring it along to show Terry Swan—but of course now, after meeting Terry, he understood why she had left it in the car; he knew, too, that she would probably not want to go to the Plaza now; it would be dullsville or squaresville; he supposed this place with the animal name would cost an arm and a leg; the $103 he had with him wouldn't take him through the Rabbit Hop.

He should have gotten more out of Hagerman; he probably could have gotten $200. The thing was he had felt sorry for Hagerman; wasn't *that* a pistol? But he had; frightened people always moved him.

When he was very young and all wrapped up in insect and animal life, and that was pretty much his world for a long time, until he was thirteen, fourteen, he had brooded over his mother's penchant for furs, imagining the terror of lacerated animals screaming in newly sprung traps. He had lain awake at night flinching in the darkness of his bedroom as he pondered the barbarism of the vivisection laboratory and the slaughterhouses. He was the bringer-home of stray cats and dogs and birds that had fallen from trees; he spent whole Saturdays and Sundays and afternoons after school tracking Billy, for Billy swung the other way; Billy was the other side of the coin. He tied cats' legs together with complicated knots and shot at chipmunks and squirrels, indifferent to whether or not he had made a clean kill, and he tortured caterpillars and angleworms and chameleons and butterflies with pins and matches, and when Charles first heard that Billy's own body was punished by the very same machinery which Billy had used to run down muskrats, kittens, raccoons, anything upon the road at night and dazzled dumbstruck by his headlights, he had not been glad—

that was not accurate—but it had not been sad news exactly;
it had made Charles believe, almost, there was a God, or
anyway, a scheme to things.

In Charles's middle teens, this emotion was transferred to
people, not so much to people he was close to, whoever they
might be—who? His mother? His father? Not the glob of
protoplasm at Holy Child, thank you; but there were a few,
as he had grown up, to whom he was close: some fellows,
the kind who hung out at the library after school or stayed
to do lab work because it interested them, the worker bees,
bespectacled and boring to any but their own kind and
their mothers. These were not the ones who touched him,
even when there was occasion to sympathize with them, a
reason—for Charles felt that they, like he, could handle
what was handed them, were strong, could take it. Hadn't he?
Lord knows what had happened to Billy was test enough
for any man, and then some, too: the way his mother had
carried on and never stopped carrying on; Charles had
watched his father lose in her eyes for the simple reason
that the well was running dry.

"Clinton, I didn't expect a lot when I married you, but I
never expected we'd be poor."

"You never expected we wouldn't be rich."

"What's the difference?"

She really didn't know.'

All right. Closest he could come to feeling sorry for someone to whom he was close was his mother; close only because she was his mother, he supposed, and yet there had
been many times in the long-ago past when he was small and
he had run to her, and she had seemed to be all there was
that mattered, that strange little woman who spoke of Jackie
as though she were a girl friend who helped give her home
perms, and not the late President's wife.

But the ones he really felt sorry for were the ones who
were scared: they were in between the ones who walked cock-
sure and sung aloud on city streets, and those who slumped
in doorways soaking in their own urine; they were not the
far-out frightened either, who wore gloves to touch money
and wiped off the silverware in restaurants before eating with
it; they were not the easily frightened who knew by heart the
telephone numbers of a drug store, police precinct, ambulance
service, and fire station.

They were the ones whose work suddenly fell out of their
hands, the ones who could not believe that it was impossible

to pick up the coffee cup because the coffee was splashing over the sides, the ones who had to sit down for a moment to remember where it was they were hurrying to, and the ones like Hagerman who had accepted it all so calmly, who had come prepared to pay off and even to toast his misfortune with a drink, only to suddenly snap a moment before preparing the drink, and kick the picnic hamper with his eyes ablaze with rage, and for one-half a second stop, bite his knuckles, pale and shaken, and then, the moment ended, run.

And Lois . . . was she one like that? Or was it all an act with her? Or both?

And now he felt so estranged from her, a way he had never felt before with her, which had never occurred to him before—that he was somewhere on the fringe of her life, on the outskirts of Lois Faye, that this place, this apartment, was very familiar to her, and the girl, Terry Swan; and all the rest was very far away, the slow hours of drinking and talking and listening to the music in Grandview Park, the ride down Route 9W to the Bluebird, the wonder of whether or not she would, wouldn't; and when she did, the soft feel of her flesh, her hands cupping her breasts to fix them for him to have, the wet answer she never failed to give him, the easy in and out and how their eyes would drink each other in, and what a way to feel; and when she didn't, how it hurt right in his guts, right there near his pancreas, knots that only she could tie. which was also something one had to grant her; he did, anyway.

Well, if she were one like that, she did not seem too scared right now. Charles heard her laughter, and the repeated "darlings" and "divines" and wandering back to pick his drink up from the kitchen counter, he stood a moment listening.

". . . really, darling, you ought to know by now I couldn't care less, darling, if you wear Celui. It's a perfect scent for you, it *really* is."

"He's out-of-whack; he never gets things right. I wear L'Heure Bleu."

"Oh, darling. I don't care."

"But, darling, I wouldn't wear your scent; now, please."

"I really don't care, I'm not that way."

"I'd never do that to anyone."

Really.

Charles looked up to the ceiling and rolled his eyes, and

was about to walk in then and join them, when he heard Terry Swan say, "Can't you get rid of Joe College?"

"You hate him, don't you?"

"I don't hate him."

"Yes you do, I know you do."

"It's just that he's not right for this crowd. This isn't **my** tame set dropping by, darling."

"Charles can be fun. After a few drinks—"

"Darling, look. Monti Rock is coming and Tiger Morse and Jerry Foyster; Andy Warhol might drop in; that's the scene, darling."

"They're coming here?"

"No. They'll be at the Cheetah. It's that kind of a scene."

"Who's coming here?"

"A few friends, very insville. One of them wants to name a racehorse after me. And *he* has a friend who's in the shipping business. He's not Onassis, but you're getting warm. And there's a broker, and another businessman."

"I'd love to meet them!"

"Shake Clyde College."

"How?"

"Can't you tell him to get lost?"

"No."

"That's right; he's your alchemist. Okay, what's *his* story? Is he a budding playwright? You could tell him you absolutely insist that he go see some play you've already seen."

"He doesn't like plays, I don't think."

"Music?"

"No, I won't be able to do that. He lives here. He's not impressed by the city."

"Did you say he lives here?"

"Yes. On East Eighty-second Street."

"He has family here?"

"Yes."

"That does it, then. Tell him you want him to stop in and say hello to his family. Tell him you wouldn't respect him, if he didn't."

"He won't fall for that, Swanny."

"Try it. Tell him you feel guilty; you want him to stop in for an hour, at least, and see his family. He can meet us at the Cheetah later."

"In an hour?"

"No, darling. We'll ditch him for three or four hours. We'll say we're eating over at the Mayfair, and that we'll meet him there. But we won't eat there. He'll come to the Cheetah eventually; he knows we're going there."

"It's awfully unkind."

"Oh, darling, he's so nowhere."

"He is?"

"Look, Lois, he's cute. God, he's very cute. I'd like to string him for a lamp. But honey, he isn't with it. That's what's wrong with chemistry. It can happen with a fry cook, for God's sake."

"He's not *that* bad!"

"Darling, Lotus. look, I'm not insulting your boyfriend; he's very cute, and I can see where you'd hear some music there, but really, sweetie, it's that strange little high music no one else hears—but dogs, maybe. Tell him to go visit his family."

Charles heard Lois sigh; then he heard Swanny dancing around the room again singing: "They Didn't Believe Me," along with Dinah Washington, and Charles shrugged and screwed up his courage, and walked in with his drink, and took his chances.

He said, "Lois, can I ask you something?"

"What?"

"In private."

"Your lips, your eyes, your dough, your hair, is in a class beyond compare, you're the most beautiful man I've ever rolled," Swanny was singing.

Lois followed him into the kitchen.

She said, "She just says things like that to shock people. She's never rolled a man in her life."

"I was thinking: I have to get my mother an Easter gift. I ought to find out from my father what she wants."

"I know what *I* want."

"You just got your Easter gift."

"I still know what I want for Easter."

"Anyway—I was thinking. Would you mind if I left you here? I could meet you later." He hoped for an explosion, an "I certainly *would* mind."

She was wrapping a strand of her hair around her first finger; she said, "I want something from the Kaleidoscope, and I want it to be vinyl."

"It *is* Celui you wear, isn't it?" He laughed; now he could not fathom her not coming with him; this was their day; all of it had been for her.

"This is *my* apartment, too," she said, "but it's a secret,

for she is suffering from a serious mental illness and has not
long to live. She thinks she's me."

"Did you hear what I said?"

"You want to leave me here."

"Unless you want to come with me. We could go to the
Plaza for drinks, the way we planned, and then we could
have dinner someplace, maybe up in the Eighties."

"Some cheap Charley's."

"No, I'll take you someplace nice. *You* can decide. But
remember what you've got on. We can't go every place."

He loved the crazy purple pants and the yellow sweater.
A poor boy, slipped over her head, became a very rich boy.

"Charles?"

"What?"

"Will you meet us later?"

In the other room, Swanny was singing. "And when you
tell them, and you're certainly going to tell them, that I'm
the broad who took your loot from you, they'll never believe
you, the fuzz won't believe you—"

"Will you, Charles? She's really very nice. She just likes to
pretend she's taking every man in pants for his money."

"She *took* the South American, didn't she?"

"What do *you* care?"

"I don't. I just want you to come with me. Don't you want
to come with me?"

"Of course I *want* to!"

"Then come."

"I can't and you know I can't! I can't be rude to my best
friend!"

"What about me?"

"I'd feel *very* guilty if you didn't go see your family
while you're in New York."

"You surprise me at times. It's sweet of you to think of
my folks."

"What kind of a girl do you think I am?"

The phone rang then. It didn't ring; it made the same ding-
dong sound as a doorbell, but Terry Swan flew into the
kitchen and picked up the small blue Princess sitting on the
counter, and said, "Hel-*lo*, there."

Lois said, "I love a bell chime. When I get my own apartment I'm going to have a bell chime."

Swanny was saying, "Oh, darling, I'm *sorry*! My mother's
ill and I have to visit her tonight."

Lois put her hand over her mouth to stifle a giggle.

Charles went into the living room and got his overcoat from the closet; the closet was lined with wallpaper which depicted a genteel demoiselle handing a flower to a kneeling knight.

He put on his coat and stood there for a moment, hoping Lois would come in from the kitchen.

But Terry Swan had hung up on her caller. She was telling Lois, "*That* was this awful man who manufactures ant farms; he *claims* he's only forty-eight, darling, but he *looks* like he's taken his first step out of Shangri-La, and he wears those Countess Mara ties that blind you with all the swirls and curlicues, and he cuts all his meat up in teeny little pieces before he eats, no matter *where* you are, Twenty-one or Clos Normand, I could just die of embarrassment, but he has tickets to everything and he's very big in the world of little gifties from Tiffany's, so I'm very sweet when he calls and—"

Charles left.

Eleven

Really, Peter Hagerman was celebrating.
In the Unmuzzled Ox.
Near ten o'clock, on the night of the Inferno.

> You are a man
> If you have a beer,
> You are a fear-less
> Care-less
> Chug-a-lug man of the
> Dia-mond.
> Clink your glass!
> Drink your glass!
> Call for more beer!
> Beer here!

Because he had had a very close call early this afternoon.
Look at it this way: there were 150 micrograms of d-lysergic acid diethylamide tartrate in each sugar cube. He had put all four, wrapped in Saran Wrap, into the thermos. If they had not fallen out of their wrappings and melted into the ice cubes en route to his rendezvous with Shepley; if things had worked out the way he had planned them, and he had slipped the sugar cubes into Shepley's drink, Shepley would probably be ape now in Rockland State booby hatch.
Which was what Hagerman had hoped for, before reason

had done battle with his rage: he had hoped to make Shepley flip, *really* flip. It had been planned very carefully; up to a point, it had gone over as though they had rehearsed:

"I hope some of the brothers saw you packing up the hamper, Shepley."

"I saw to it. But it was a pain in the ass lugging it out here."

"Oh, you have it rough, man! I'm going to be out a hundred and fifty dollars, and you gripe about lugging a picnic hamper out on the bus. You did take the bus?"

"No, I flew. I'm Superpledge."

"Well, Shep, you pulled a pretty super swindle on me."

"You asked for it."

"You're right. Shep, I've cooled down since our little talk. You may think I'm still p.o.'d, but I have to hand it to you. You've got guts."

"And I'm not going to back down, Hagerman."

"Hell, is that what you think I think? You think I think that? I know when I'm licked."

"Then let's get it over with."

"I've got to stall for about fifteen minutes. Some of the other actives are down the road. I want to wait until they go before I take off. See, they think I'm up here making you go through all kinds of hell. See, I've got to maintain my image, mother-lover."

"Yeah. Your image."

"I'm not a bad egg when you get to know me, Shep. Want a drink?"

"All right."

"We'll toast your initiative, want to? Are there paper cups in the hamper?"

"Yeah, but what's *that*?"

"It's port."

"*Port?*"

"Hell, it's good stuff. Sandeman's Tawny."

"Isn't that a little sweet?"

"I've got some ice to cut it. If you don't want it, well—"

"I suppose I can choke it down."

"Let me get us some ice from the thermos."

"Hagerman?"

"What?"

"Why don't we get the business over with first?"

"Sure, Shep."

They had made the exchange: a roll of tape for a roll of

bills; then Hagerman had gone over and picked the thermos up from the ground, and unscrewed the lid.

The sugar cubes were dissolved, so was the dream of Shepley going off his rocker, going so far off his rocker he'd wind up like someone who'd had a lobotomy performed on him; if six hundred micrograms of the stuff couldn't do that, rain couldn't get you wet.

There would be nothing to fear from Shepley again, nor from Blouter.

But it had not worked out, had it? And really, Hagerman was celebrating. He really was. He was singing all the old Pi Pi songs—he knew them all by heart, all the verses of all of them, and he was teaching them to Thorpe who was so pie-eyed his head was hanging by a thread, and he had put Charles Shepley clear out of his mind; the boy didn't exist, that was a fact.

Thorpe was talking about some goddam girl and how they used Saran Wrap when they made out, and even the mention of Saran Wrap did not bug Hagerman.

Nothing could.

Not even Old Len and Peg Beauty, if they were to stroll in arm-in-arm wearing sandwich boards with Greecemark written on them.

Hagerman ordered another round of beer. Then he got up and went back to the phone booth, and by now he knew the number by heart, so he just closed the door and slipped a dime down the slot, and dialed.

"Hello?"

"The Congs are going to kill Turtle."

He waited for the click and the dial tone, but this time she didn't hang up.

She said, "Why do you think so?"

"Because you never gave a *damn* about him, Matilda!"

"How do *you* know that?"

Hagerman was not stupid; she was trying to hold him on the line so the call could be traced. Well, *that* took time.

Hagerman said. "What kind of encouragement did you ever give him, Matilda?"

"I love Joey. He's my only son."

"Your only son. Tch, tch, tch. I'm impressed."

"Why do you want to torment me?"

"You tormented *him,* didn't you? You underestimated *him,* didn't you?"

"You read the piece in *The Far Point Record,* is that right?"

"Victor Charlie's captured him. Matilda; he's being tortured right now. If you listen real hard, you can hear him screaming . . . Yeeeowww!"

He hung up.

When he went back to the booth and sat down, Thorpe said, "It must be hard with Janish so far away. You mish her?"

Then Thorpe's head hit the table; the beer glass smashed to the floor, and a waiter hustled over.

"Eighty-six," he said.

Really, Peter Hagerman was invulnerable.

"I apologize for my companion," he said. He said, "Come on, pledge, let's call it a night."

With the waiter's help, Hagerman got Thorpe out into the street. At the curb, Thorpe vomited.

Hagerman waited it out patiently. Then he got Thorpe into the car, and he drove him down Route 9W to a Mobil station. He steered him into the rest room, where Thorpe got sick again.

"Clean yourself up," said Hagerman. "I'll wait outside."

There was just enough time for Hagerman to step into the phone booth and pay the dime and hear Matilda Holt's hello.

Said Hagerman, "Yeeeeeeeeowwwwwwwwwww!"

Then he went inside and bought a ginger ale from the vending machine, and handed it to Thorpe, when Thorpe came out of the men's.

"Soothe your tum-tum," he said, handing it to Thorpe, smiling.

Bud Burroughs said to his mother, "You make the best mashed potatoes in the world!"

"I don't use mixes. You want another helping, dear?"

"Thanks . . . It's more than not using mixes. We don't use mixes at the house, but ours don't taste like this."

"I put a little sour cream in. And lots of butter."

"They sure are good."

"Then you should come home more often, Buddy."

"Oh, Mom, you know how that would look. Running home to my mother. Anyway, I have to pay for the meal whether I'm there or not; I might as well get my money's worth. Or Dad's money's worth."

"I wonder where your father is? He went off duty two hours ago. It's almost ten o'clock."

"He's probably out collecting graft from the local bars."

"Buddy, I don't like that talk."

"I'm only *kidding*."

"There's not a policeman in this state as honest as your father."

"Hopkins would be pleased to hear that."

"Dick Hopkins is honest, too. I don't know any who aren't."

"Mom, I was only kidding."

"You're always saying things like that, though; they aren't funny, Buddy. There's nothing funny about them."

"Okay, I won't say them anymore."

"I think it's that roommate of yours, that Hagerman. I think he puts ideas in your head."

"You've never even met him."

"I wish you'd bring him home. I'd like to meet him."

"Mom, I told you—he's not an average guy. You'd be uncomfortable, and he'd be uncomfortable. . . . He's sort of cynical. You know?"

"I just have to listen to you to know."

"But he's a nice guy. Take tonight. You know, it's Hell Night at the frat. Well, Peter knows I'm not good at that kind of stuff; you know, ordering the pledges to do these crazy stunts. He lets me skip it. All the other actives have to do it—that's why there's no dinner at the house tonight. But Peter lets me off."

"I thought Hell Night was against the college rules."

"Oh, *Mom!*"

"Isn't Hell Night against the college rules?"

"Mom, can't you ever forget about rules and laws; is that all you worry about, rules and laws?"

"I respect rules and laws, Buddy."

"I respect your fine, rich, thick, country-style brown gravy. May I have some more?"

"Oh, *you!*"

She laughed, and picked up the gravy bowl, and carried it into the kitchen.

Then Arnold Burroughs came in the front door and called out, "It's me!" as he did every night of his life, and Bud's mother called back, "Is that you, dear?" as she did every night, and Arnold Burroughs answered, "I'm home."

Bud Burroughs said, "How do you two ever remember all that?"

"Hi, Buddy! All what?"

"You know. It's me. Is that you, dear? I'm home."

His father mussed Bud's hair playfully and said, "It took twenty-three years of practice. Who let you out of prison?"

"It's Hell Night. I'm too much of an angel to participate."

"What do you mean it's Hell Night?" His father's smile vanished, and he stood there without removing his coat, waiting for an answer.

"Now don't *you* start, Dad. You know darn well the frats still take their pledges out for fun and games. It's really just one night. Just one night."

"Like tonight?"

"Yeah. You going to arrest them or something? Take your coat off."

Arnold Burroughs took off his coat, but he didn't walk to the closet with it; he pulled up a chair next to Bud and sat down. He said, "Is tonight the night?"

"Yeah."

"Maybe there *is* something to it."

"Something to what?"

"We thought we had a psycho on our hands, but maybe there *is* something to it."

"To *what?*"

"Are the eggheads in this fraternity you belong to against the war in Vietnam?"

"Some of them are, I suppose."

"Anyone in particular?"

"I didn't take a poll."

"Bud, don't give me any of your wise-guy answers; we've got a serious situation on our hands."

"What is it?"

Then Burroughs' father told him about Matilda Holt, and her drunken visitor, and the subsequent obscene phone calls that were continuing even as Arnold Burroughs had left the station.

Ida Burroughs had joined them around the dinner table, and she was shaking her head and exclaiming "Oh, *no!*" at intervals, and when her husband had finished, she looked across at Bud and said, "You see?"

"Do I see what?"

"What we were talking about earlier. About respect for rules and laws."

"Mom, for Pete's sake! Nobody from Pi Pi would do a thing like this! For Pete's sake!"

"If it is someone from that fraternity of yours, mister, you've spent your last day there!" said Arnold Burroughs. "But it isn't!"

"Well, I don't like to think it is. But you tell me it's fun-and-games night, and this happens the same night. And the boy told Mrs. Holt that he was from the college."

Bud Burroughs gave an exasperated sigh. "Do you think that someone from the college would *say* he was from the college?"

"Well, I didn't think so when I heard it, but I didn't know this was some sort of special Halloween at your place, either."

"Dad!"

"And the boy *was* drunk. Mrs. Holt said he could hardly walk. He might not have known what he was saying."

"It's nobody from Pi Pi, I can tell you that."

"We haven't had any other complaints; where are your Pi Pis?"

"They're not running wild in the streets ringing Mrs. Holt's doorbell."

"This boy was in a car."

"Did she get the license number?"

"She was too upset. She didn't even know what color the car was."

"Everything that goes wrong in this town gets hung on the college."

"We give you kids a lot of leeway, Bud."

"Anyway," said Ida Burroughs, "I'm glad Buddy isn't involved. He was here all night, and I can swear to that."

"Mother, no one from the fraternity or the college was involved! How about the high school kids in this town? I did some pretty wild things when *I* was in high school."

"High school kids aren't driving around in cars after six at night."

"Oh, that's really using your head, Dad. If they're drunk, why aren't they driving around after six? You mean, because it'd be breaking the law?"

Arnold Burroughs slammed his fist down on the table, rattling the plates and silverware, sloshing the milk in Bud's glass over the side. He said, "Look, Bud, I've had enough of your sarcasm! I didn't work overtime, trying to help some woman who's frightened out of her wits to come home to a fresh kid who thinks the Far Point police are a bunch of fatheads! That's what you think, isn't it?"

"No, Dad."

Ida Burroughs said, "You see, Buddy? You go too far."

"I'm sorry. I really am."

"Well, you put this in your pipe and smoke it, Buddy! If this *has* got anything to do with the monkeyshines those Little Lord Fauntleroys you live with classify as fun-and-games, you're going to be classified as a dropout quicker than you can say Pi Pi! You're going to college to get an education; you're privileged to live in a fraternity where you can learn to be a gentleman, but you're not privileged to be a Vietnik, or a beatnik, or any other nutnik! Do you understand, Bud?"

Ida Burroughs said, "*He* didn't do anything, Arnie. He was here with me all night."

"Do you understand, Bud?"

"Yes, sir."

"I don't want to hear about you or anyone you know causing harm to anyone. If I hear you or anyone you know caused harm to anyone, I'll put you down on the assembly line at F.P.B. . . . And that goes for tonight, a year from tonight, or four years from tonight!"

"Yes, sir."

"The whole damn lot of you ought to live through one hour of what our boys live through every day in Vietnam; then you'd really know something about hell!"

Ida Burroughs said, "Now, Arnie, you don't mean that."

"I mean it all right, and Bud knows I mean it!"

"Yes," Burroughs said, "I know you mean it."

That night when Bud Burroughs returned to the Pi Pi house, before he did anything else he went up to his room and got Peter's keys to the refrigerator and Peter's medicine case. He was not surprised to find the four sugar cubes in the case, where Peter had promised to put them, but he was relieved by his decision to destroy them. So much for the likelihood of his causing anyone any harm; so much for his experiment. No one would be any the worse for it now. . . . Nor would anyone have been any the worse for what Bud flushed down the Pi Pi toilet. Four ordinary Dominoes couldn't hurt a fly.

Twelve

Earlier that evening, the blinking blue light above the telephone in Clinton Shepley's laboratory signaled that someone was on the line. Shepley glanced up, annoyed. Before the interruption, his thin six-foot frame had been hunched over a breeding case, his dark eyes fixed on two praying mantes. As Shepley picked up the arm of the phone, the female decapitated the male, while the male continued to hold his amorous posture on her.

"Shepley speaking."

"Shepley speaking," said the voice.

"Charles!"

"Hi, Dad."

"Where are you?"

"At the reception desk. May I come up?"

"Of course!"

"I'll be right up."

Clinton Shepley put down the receiver and glanced at his wristwatch; it was ten minutes to seven.

He made a note of the number of males the female mantis had devoured, and then switched off the show lights in the breeding case. He fished in the pocket of his lab coat for a cigarette, scratched a match against a wooden bench, and walked to the window, sucking in the smoke.

He had been with the institute for twenty-five years, counting those years when he was on leave of absence during World War II. He had had several opportunities, before Billy's accident, to leave the institute for more remunerative positions, but there had always been the extra money from his father's estate. Now, with the expense of Billy's illness eating that up, Clinton Shepley's income was barely adequate. There was compensation in the knowledge that, given two or three more years he hoped to have the most definitive information ever collected concerning the mating habits of invertebrates; there was even more recompense in the fact he was doing the work he did best, and the Richmond Institute was the only place where he could accomplish it.

But he was not a bachelor, like old Stanchfield in Reptiles, who was going into his eleventh year of a study on venomous tree snakes, nor was Natalie very much like Wendt's wife, who followed him into the sea in pursuit of information about the nest structures of Poikilotherms.

If he had married anyone but a woman like Natalie, Billy's illness might have seemed a tragedy which they could, thank God, afford, but instead, it was a tragedy which deprived them of the things Natalie had counted on in their marriage, and every day Clinton Shepley was reminded of this fact.

"You want to hear my nightmare, Clint?" she had said that morning at breakfast, before the call from Charles.

"All right."

"You and I were out at dinner and it was a very fancy restaurant, and you ordered dinner for us. Remember that time we went to Le Provençal?"

"Vaguely."

"*Vaguely?* On East Sixty-second Street, remember? I was all gussied up and we sat at a little table in the back. Billy must have been about thirteen, because I remember he was old enough to sit with Charles, so we didn't have a sitter, and it was winter, I remember, because it was snowing."

"What has that got to do with your nightmare, Natalie?"

"In my nightmare, we were in the same kind of restaurant. I mean, it might even have been Le Provençal. It probably was. You ordered dinner. I remember that part, except I don't remember what we had for a main course. The entrée. That part I don't recall. I recall that we started with Quiche Lorraine. Guess what we drank."

"What did we drink?"

"Taittinger Blanc de Blancs 1959. That was right in my nightmare."

"Why was it a nightmare?"

"I'm getting to that, Clint! We started with Quiche Lorraine and Taittinger Blanc de Blancs 1959, and we finished with soufflé Grand Marnier, accompanied by those enormous strawberries with cream on them. They were as big as plums. And the wine steward brought us Moët et Chandon Dom Perignon 1959. That was right in my nightmare, the year and everything . . . Well, my teeth fell out."

"I see."

"It may not sound like much, but they began falling out when the waiter put down the Quiche Lorraine, and I kept putting them one by one into my handkerchief, and by the time the strawberries came, I didn't have a tooth in my mouth. Can you imagine how I felt?"

"What did you do, gum your strawberries?"

"I know it *sounds* funny, Clint, but I woke up with goose bumps all over my body. I had to turn on Long John to quiet me down, and his whole program was about the Jet Set. Well, I guess the only Jet Set we qualify for anymore is the Jim Dooley Jet Set."

"Were we in the Jet Set? I hadn't realized."

"We went to Paris."

"What's the Jim Dooley Jet Set?"

"New York to Miami. Come on down! Hi, Brooklyn! Hello, Five forty-two Lexington! Haven't you ever seen him on television?"

"I'm sorry you had a nightmare."

"When Billy's better, I want to go to Acapulco; that's the 'in' place now."

"Well. When Billy's better, it might not be the 'in' place anymore. By then, the moon might be the 'in' place, Natalie."

"If I didn't believe Billy was going to get well, I wouldn't be able to keep on living like this, Clint."

The institute overlooked the East River, with its Pearl-Wick Hampers and Pepsi-Cola signs, and the tugs that glided past, and in the distance the smoke from the factories of Queens, the beginnings of Long Island, the lights of the bridge and traffic stealing back and forth across it. Clinton Shepley liked the view, even the advertisements amused him; he liked the whole neighborhood of the institute, and he was glad when his financial circumstances forced the move here from Riverside Drive.

Natalie was always harping on the fact that the outdoor phone booths on East End Avenue were broken into nearly every night, and that the dope addicts who were involved in the Janice Wylie murder case had lived only two blocks away from their apartment, but the neighborhood held many good memories for Clinton Shepley, not the least of which were memories of his walks with Charles along the promenade by the East River.

When Charles was a youngster, he was always dropping in at the institute after school and on Saturdays. Billy had rarely shown any interest in the place; he showed up only when he wanted to borrow a few dollars. But Charles had genuinely loved watching the experiments; he used to sit for hours with Clinton Shepley waiting for a Callinecte to attract a female, or for a gray Sepia to come up from the mud and change its color to purple-black stripes for the female, or for a wolf spider to complete his dance around his mate.

During their walks along the promenade, Charles would talk of his ambition to be a zoologist, and what branch of the science he wanted to concentrate on, and what college he thought offered the most. But the conversation was not limited to that; in Charles, Clinton Shepley found what he missed with Natalie, the easy rapport which lent itself to discussions of people—Charles telling of this boy in his class, or that teacher—Clinton Shepley regaling Charles with stories of Stanchfield's habit of favoring certain snakes by allowing them to sleep nights in his bathroom, and of Wendt's wife climbing a tree to sketch the foam nest of a Polypedates rheinwartii, only to come hysterically upon a bag of bats. . . . They were boon companions, Clinton Shepley and his younger son.

But a change had come over Charles after Billy's accident; it showed first in his grades, and ultimately in his estrangement from his father. He was polite, but distant; attentive when Clinton Shepley discussed things with him, but unenthusiastic. Around this period, too, he picked up this knack for imitating people; he was very good at it. Even his face seemed to take on the features of the person he was mimicking. It became very hard to find Charles beneath them all.

While Clinton Shepley waited for his son to come up to

the laboratory, he felt the same apprehension he had after his telephone conversation that morning. He should not have lied to Charles; he probably wouldn't have told the old Charles a lie; he might have been able to make that Charles see some humor in Natalie Shepley's pathetic maneuver, or at least help him see how pathetic it was. But now he was so out of touch with his son; and the knowledge of the promise of silverware had come as a shock to Clinton Shepley, as well.

Of course it was the reason for Charles's visit; in minutes, there would be the confrontation, and what was he to tell the boy?

He might begin by saying, "You see, Charles, it wasn't so much your mother's fear for you—that's only the superficial motivation, but go deeper. She projects her fears onto me and you and even onto Billy. Charles," chuckling? "she even sent away to one of those mail order houses for a phony family coat of arms to hang in Billy's room to impress the nuns with his lineage."

But that would hardly undo the damage, would it? She had made a fool of him in the eyes of his fraternity; what was there to say to make *that* less humiliating?

Clinton Shepley took a last drag on his cigarette, ground out the stub in the ash tray, and waited for his son without the slightest notion of how to handle the situation.

But the situation was not the one he was expecting.

Charles Shepley had also had time to reflect on the past, on the hours he had spent with his father at the institute, their walks along the promenade, the way it used to be; he had thought of little else during his ride up from Fifty-seventh Street on the Third Avenue bus, and his leisurely walk across to East End Avenue.

Suddenly, he had come to. It was 1966, and he was nineteen years old, and the past five years were at an end, and this was the beginning of where he had left off. And he *did* care that Lois Faye had chosen to stay at Terry's; he did and would maybe for a long time want that girl so badly that he could conjure up the sensation of having her, and feel the sensation prick the flesh of his fingertips, and feel his insides do a loop, but he did not care, not any longer, enough to exist for that and that alone. Nor was he as he had been before he met her, the only non-astronaut who could hang in space weightless, floating around like a gas balloon with an endless supply of helium.

"I hope I didn't interrupt something important, Dad."

"You didn't. It's good to see you, Charles."

They shook hands, and Charles removed his overcoat. While his father was hanging it up in the lab closet, Charles snapped on the light in the mantes' breeding case.

"Is this Lolita? I remember you writing me about her."

"No, that's Lynda Bird. She just destroyed George Hamilton; he was her sixth suitor."

"Poor George. Lost his head, hmmm?"

"All seven did."

"Does decapitation actually make the male mantis more potent? I read that somewhere."

"That's the theory. Of course, science is always turning up evidence that the male in lower organisms is superfluous."

"The other night I was thinking about those lizards that reproduce themselves by parthenogenesis. Cnemidophorus tessellatus, isn't that the name?"

"Yes. I didn't know you were still interested in all this."

"I haven't been for awhile, but I'd like to get back to it."

"Would you, Charles?"

"Yes."

"I'm delighted to hear it!"

"Of course, Far Point isn't the best college for what I want."

His father pulled up a lab stool and sat beside him; he said, "And you're thinking of leaving, is that it?"

"No."

Charles's father looked surprised. Charles said, "A quitter never wins, and a winner never quits; isn't that what you always used to say?" He grinned at his father. "You were a real corn ball, weren't you?"

"What do you mean I *was*? I still am."

"I remember a lot of *your* old platitudes: keep on keeping on; if someone hands you a lemon, squeeze it and start a lemonade stand: a year from now, what will I regret not having done today?; when you're through learning, you're through; you have two duties—to worry, and not to worry; happiness makes up in height for what it lacks in length. . . . *You* were full of them. But I only remember Mom saying one."

"What was that?"

"Money is honey, my little sonny, and a rich man's joke is always funny. Remember?"

They both laughed.

"She still says it, all the time," said Charles's father.

"I think it made a dent," Charles said, "I think I took a ride on it for a while."

"What do you mean, Charles?"

"Well, I figured if I couldn't have the best, I didn't want second best."

"You mean Princeton? You could have gone to Princeton, Charles. Your grades kept you out of Princeton."

"I know it. But all her talk about money got to me, I think. I think I felt she'd resent it if I went to such an expensive school. Or maybe I just used that for an excuse to just give up . . . I don't know."

His father lit a cigarette. He said, "I never understood why you lost your interest in school after Billy's accident."

"I guess I felt sorry for myself. I thought I was going to have my own car, like Billy did, and go to Princeton—"

His father interrupted, "Where students can't have their own cars."

Charles snickered. "Is that a fact?"

"They get around on bicycles."

Charles hit his forehead with his palm, "Well, that's what I mean. I *didn't* think . . . Anyway, the wheels are beginning to turn again. They aren't going full speed yet, but they're starting. I'd like to talk about it with you, Dad."

"I'd like that, too."

"Do you suppose Mom can afford to feed another mouth tonight?"

Natalie Shepley did not drink very much; when she did, she went the Cherry Heering, Tia Maria, crème de menthe, Grand Marnier route. She really did not like the taste of whiskey or gin or rum or vodka. But with ginger ale, whiskey went down very smoothly, and she *did* collect fancy whiskey containers. She had them in various shapes: a boat, a frog, a clock, an airplane, a dwarf, a Christmas tree, and now a bottle of Dickel whiskey in the shape of a powder horn.

Clint had called from the institute around seven fifteen and said Charles was there and coming home with Clint for dinner, and they were going to stop for some liquor; what would she like?

She said, "Does that mean Charles isn't coming home for Easter, Clint?"

"I don't know, Natalie."

"I bet that's what it means. I told Billy he was coming, too."

"Billy will forgive him, Natalie."

"You don't believe that; you don't even believe Billy hears what I tell him."

"Do you want some Cherry Heering?"

"I haven't had anything new for my collection for months, not since Ken Wendt was here for dinner."

"I was only thinking of you."

"I can drink whiskey."

"All right, Natalie. Now don't mention the silverware thing."

"Do you think I *would?* You don't think I have any feelings, do you, Clint?"

"I know you have very strong feelings."

"The nuns say they don't know how I hold up the way I do."

"We'll see you soon, dear."

It was ten o'clock now; the dishes were rinsed off and put into the dishwasher, and Charles and his father were still sitting at the dinner table over coffee.

Natalie Shepley went into the dining room, carrying a mason jar. She took the powder horn from the center of the table, and began pouring the whiskey into the jar.

"Natalie, *what* are you doing?"

"I'm going to rinse out my powder horn and put it with my collection."

"Can't you wait until we're finished?"

"You have a lot to talk about, and I can't even start the dishwasher because you complain about the noise. That's what I hate about having an apartment where the dining room is right on top of the kitchen . . . I'm not bothering you, am I?"

Clinton Shepley sighed. He said, "It isn't very gracious pouring a drink from a mason jar, but go ahead; you've done it now."

"This has been such a gracious evening, too."

Charles said, "What's the matter, Mom?" and those four little words opened the floodgates.

"Oh *no!*" Clinton Shepley groaned. "Not tonight, Natalie."

But tonight was no different from any other night when Natalie Shepley drank whiskey, for a bottle of whiskey, whether it was in the shape of a winter flounder or a surrey, was really a Pandora's box, out of which flew their balance at Bankers Trust, Billy, the nightmare of her teeth falling out at Le Provençal, all the Carter Burden parties they would never attend, a neighborhood housing dope addicts who tied girls together and committed obscene acts upon them, and no one but nuns to appreciate her.

Natalie Shepley ran down the hall and into the bathroom, where she grabbed a wad of Kleenex and wailed.

Then she opened the door a crack, and she heard Clint saying, ". . . wrong with her but one too many."

Charles said, "I guess it's rough on her, though."

Which set her off again, for ten seconds more, during which she also blew her nose and ran a comb through her hair. Then she went into the bedroom and sat down in the noiseless swivel rocker, and put her hands across her face in a gesture of despair, and waited for Charles to come.

Charles took his time about it, but that was Clint's doing, because she could hear Clint saying, "She'll get over it," and "She's all right."

She was not all right, and she was tired of putting on a good face and pretending that she was all right, and it was high time someone besides the sisters at Holy Child realized it, so she told Charles about it when he finally appeared, pulling up a footstool and trying to jolly her.

"I know it's rough, Mom. I know," he said.

"I tried to make everything nice, and you didn't even notice. You didn't even notice the hollandaise. It wasn't out of a jar, if you think it was."

"It was very good. It was very selfish of me not to mention it."

"You don't mean to be selfish, but you're like your father."

"Mom, we both loved the dinner. Did we leave anything on our plates? Didn't we have second helpings?"

"It isn't just the dinner. It's everything. I'm running myself ragged, Charles."

"Well, take it *easy*, Mom."

"How can I? We can't afford a full-time maid, and if I didn't go to see Billy every day, he'd just waste away there like a vegetable."

"Mom, maybe you should go every other day, instead of every day. Really, Mom."

"He's my responsibility. You don't understand responsibility. Neither does your father. Your father could have been the director of Richmond Institute; he had the seniority and everything, but he didn't want the responsibility and he doesn't understand what it is, and you don't run for office either, do you?"

"Mom, I'm a pledge. Pledges don't run for office."

"*Will* you run for office, when you're an active? You won't."

"Mom, that's not something I have to worry about right now."

"I bet Mr. Blouter worried about it when he was a pledge."

"Maybe he did."

"It isn't much, but it's something; it's better than nothing to be the president of a fraternity. Your father wasn't anything in his chapter either, but your father had money, and that makes a difference."

"Mother? How did you know Mike Blouter is our president?"

"Your letters. Your letters, Charles."

"I never mentioned Mike. I didn't."

"Then your father must have told me."

"How would Dad know?"

"Oh, Charles, does the subject of the conversation always have to go back to you? There's Billy over in Holy Child so *very* ill and you—"

But Charles did not let her finish.

He said, "Mother, did you write that letter? Did you? Did you promise the fraternity silverware if they'd pledge me?"

"Your father does not want me to discuss this subject, Charles."

"He knew about it, too? Dad knew about it, too?"

At a loss for words, Natalie Shepley decided to whimper and shiver until Charles left, which was not a long time to have to whimper and shiver, only a few seconds.

He said flatly, "Good night, Mom."

Nothing about Easter; nothing about the Pi Pi mother's pin.

Thirteen

There was a maze of lights flashing different colors; huge sheets of chrome were suspended behind the bandstand, and the booths were upholstered in fake fur.

The man with Lois Faye owned the Hi-Spray Car Wash —Coin Operated chain; he was a bachelor in his forties, and he wore a four-in-hand polka dot necktie five inches wide, with a matching pocket handkerchief, and a dark blue pin-striped suit. His name was Freddy, and he was not at all what Lois had expected, nor was Sam, Swanny's date, who wore contact lenses, worked on Wall Street, and drove an Impala, which was in a parking lot a block away from the Cheetah.

Sam kept saying they should have gone to Arthur, where they could get a drink; Cheetah served only soft drinks, wine, or beer.

"I want to see this Baby Jane what's-her-name," said Freddy. "Did you ever see her?"

Sam said, "She's old hat." He looked at Swanny and said, "Isn't she old hat?"

"Very old hat," said Swanny, who was feeling the martinis they had downed at the Mayfair.

Sam said, "He embarrasses me. He still thinks Bogey and Betty are married."

He laughed very hard at that; to be sure everyone heard

it and got it, he said, "Freddy still thinks Humphrey Bogart and Lauren Bacall are married."

Swanny said, "Play it again, Sam."

Sam guffawed and then pretended to be playing a piano.

Swanny said, "I was at Arthur last week with this Englishman, and when I asked him if he thought Prince Charlie was an alcoholic, he said the question was a little previous. *Previous*; how do you like that for openers?"

Freddy said, "I was previous for a whole week, but I'm regular again now."

Sam and Freddy howled, and Swanny looked across at Lois and made her thumb and first finger into a gun and pointed it at her forehead. But she was laughing at the same time, and she grabbed Sam's hand and said she wanted to dance, and they got up and left Lois and Freddy alone together.

Freddy said, "Last week I saw Orson Bean. At Shepheard's."

Lois said, "You like celebrities, don't you? You like them *a lot*."

"Well, sure, because in my line of business you don't meet many . . . you don't meet *any*."

Then he said, "I think it's swell that you're going to college."

"It is swell. It's swell."

"Well, it *is* swell . . . Do you want to be something?"

"What do you mean, Freddy?"

"You know, a nurse or a teacher or something?"

"I want to be a spy."

"No kidding?"

"No kidding."

"I couldn't see being a spy. I don't like to travel. My stomach acts up. Even if I take the train."

"Are you successful and have an ulcer as a result of fighting your way to the top?"

"Huh?"

"Never mind."

"I don't have an ulcer. I have colitis . . . You were just kidding me about studying to be a spy, weren't you?"

"Uh-huh."

"I thought you were . . . Do you want to trip the light fantastic?"

"All right, we might as well."

He said, "I wasn't saying that seriously; that's just a camp way of asking someone to dance. Do you know about camp?"

"Not a great deal."

"Well, it's Big Little Books and everything. It's hard to explain."

"Explain it when we sit down, okay?"

"If I can. This whole place is camp, for example," he said, as he led her onto the dance floor.

There were girls in bell-bottom lamé pants suits, giraffe-patterned culottes, mid-thigh dresses, and vinyl suits; there were young men in flannel suits with long jackets and wide lapels, in leather suits, in checkered knickers with madras vests and ice-cream-color silk shirts and floppy ties, in caps, chaps, spats, and high-heeled boots.

The music was live and loud, the lights were eerie, and everyone was gyrating and smiling, and across the room Lois saw Sam's behind wagging frantically, and in front of her Lois watched Freddy do strange little steps he had made up himself, while the perspiration rolled down his face, and he snapped his fingers and told himself "Go, boy!" at ten-second intervals.

For some reason, she thought of that night in front of the Unmuzzled Ox, when she had stood in the crowd and watched the Kappas flushing like toilets on the sidewalk, and for the first time she realized that what she had felt was envy, and that right now she felt envious of all the girls who weren't there with dates like Sam and Freddy. The race-horse owner and the shipping magnate hadn't showed.

She read very little, Lois Faye; she read the books assigned in E-Lit, and a few years ago she had read a book called *The Ski Bum*, which she had liked a lot, and she had started to read one called *The Adventurers* last summer, but there was one book she had read before any of those, a book by Carson McCullers, *The Member of the Wedding*, and there was a part she had never forgotten. It was the part when the young girl, Frankie, was jealous of some girls who had a club and would not ask her to join, and when Frankie's maid suggested she make herself president of her own club, Frankie had answered, "I don't want to be president of a lot of left-over people."

She thought of that, thought that she wasn't even president of them, just perpetually a part of them, whether at the dorm at F.P.C., or out for an evening in New York City, with Swanny who was suddenly not The One, but just another loser, no better than Freddy who cherished the memory of seeing Orson Bean at Shepheard's.

It was a dismal revelation.

When she went back to the booth with Freddy and sat down, she was in a near-catatonic state.

"Do you want a hot dog?" he said.

She shrugged.

"That's the only food they sell here. That's camp, too."

"We just ate."

"I know it, but I'm very oral, I guess. Were you ever analyzed?"

She shook her head.

"I was in for five years. It cost me eight thousand dollars! . . . I don't know, maybe it was worth it . . . Five years ago I was a real jerk. I used to go to these dansants, you know? For discriminating young singles between twenty-two and thirty-eight. Places like Ondine, and Inner Circle and the Mirror Room at Longchamps. They have them on Friday nights and Sunday afternoons, and the fellows pay two dollars. It's a good deal if you're not making much money, and in those days I didn't have Hi-Spray going for me, and a buck was a buck. *Believe* me! . . . So I went to these dansants, and I just stood around, like Marty or something. Did you see *Marty*, the movie?"

"Uh-huh."

"Well, that's what I did. I stood around like Marty. . . . So I got analyzed, and it helped my social life."

"Good."

"I keep up with things now. Like camp . . . Are you sure you don't want a hot dog?"

"*You* do, so why don't you get one?"

"Do you mind sitting here alone? I could wait until Sam and Terry get back to the table."

"I don't mind."

"Are you *sure*?"

"Yes."

He got up and pawed his way through the crowd, and Lois Faye felt close to tears.

Then suddenly, then miraculously, Lois Faye saw Charles walking toward the table. She realized she was seeing the only person with whom she wanted to be.

A half hour ago, when he had left the apartment, he had told his father, "Don't worry about it."

"But I *do* worry about it, Charles. I should have told you this afternoon when you came to the institute."

"It wasn't *your* fault."

"I shouldn't have lied to you."

"Let's just forget it."

"What are you going to do about it?"

"What *can* I do about it?"

"I'm sorry, Charles. I know it's humiliating."

"It's no skin off mine," Charles had answered.

It wasn't either. It was skin off Hagerman. It was good for a lot more than $150. He didn't need a tape now to make Blouter believe what Hagerman had said: Hagerman had been telling the truth, divulging top-secret information, not playing a mean little prank. Blouter might have forgiven a prank, but he would not forgive this. No wonder Hagerman had paid off so easily. No wonder a lot of things: no wonder Charles had been pocket-pledged the second night of Rush; no wonder Hagerman had hated him on sight; no wonder Mike had roared at Charles's imitation and called Hagerman over to hear. . . . A rich man's joke is *always* funny.

Charles sat down across from Lois.

He said, "I was just passing by. I heard the music and I saw the pictures of the girls out front, and I thought what-the-hell, you're not in the big city every day and ten cents isn't going to *break* you. Want to dance?"

"Charles, can we go?"

"What? Leave all this action? I'm rich as Croesus, and very big in the world of little gifties from Tiffany's."

"I want to go; can we go?"

"Where? El Morocco? Twenty-one? The Stork Club?"

"The *Stork* Club? The Stork Club isn't open anymore! You're such a hick!"

"Let me tell you about the ant farms I manufacture."

"Oh, Charles. I missed you. *A lot!*"

Charles smiled. There was some change on the table near his elbow. He eased his arm back until his palm made contact with it. "You didn't even know I was gone."

"I did! It was just awful, this whole evening."

"You know what time it is, don't you? The dorm closed an hour ago."

"I've already signed out."

"You *what*?"

"I was going to stay all night with Swanny."

"Was I supposed to hitchhike back?"

"Charles, I'm being honest with you, at least. I didn't *have* to tell you."

"I'm awfully glad you did. I feel great."

"It isn't easy to be honest. Give me *some* credit."

"*You* were going to stay with Swanny. We were coming in to buy you a Pucci, and have dinner, and *you* were going to stay with Swanny. I could turn into a cynic; old Docile Charlie could turn into a cynic, do you know that?"

"Charles, my date is going to come back any minute. Let's go."

"Where? Are you planning to sleep at the house?"

"You don't have to be in until three this morning! You *told* me that!"

"Where are *you* going to be at three this morning?"

"You always make me beg you to take me to the Bluebird," she said. "You like to *lord* it over me!"

Charles Shepley roared; so did Lois.

Then he slipped the change from the table into his overcoat. While she was in the ladies', Charles went to the lounge and called the Bluebird for a reservation; after that, he very gracefully pocketed a gold cigarette case he saw resting on a couch.

There was a boutique in the Cheetah. Before they left, Charles bought her a pair of backless suede boots.

"You're in a better mood than I've ever seen you in in my whole life!" she said later, as they were crossing the George Washington Bridge.

"I have some game in me," he smiled.

"*At last!*" she answered.

He was thinking that by the time he got back to the house, most of the Pi Pis would be asleep; he was thinking of Blouter's suite on the third floor, unoccupied, vulnerable, with the petty cash in a portable lockbox in Blouter's closet.

Fourteen

Thorpe said, "Have you read the morning papers, Hager-man?"

Hagerman had a hangover. He was in his room, still dressed in pajamas, swallowing down Gelusil.

He had not read the newspapers yet, but he had known what to expect. When he had come in last night, Burroughs had told him all about the police and the reporters hovering around Matilda Holt's place, and how it had inspired him to flush the sugar cubes down the john, and Hagerman had gone to sleep pleased to think that Bud would never know that Hagerman had tried to dose Shepley with them. Hagerman had wondered what would have happened if Bud had gone ahead with his experiment, and discovered the cubes were ordinary Dominoes; he would only have had to swallow one, found it produced no reaction, and then analyzed the other three.

Things had a way of working out in Hagerman's favor; now if he could just get Thorpe off his back, he could go to his classes and conduct the pledges through their Day of Purgatorio, and calm down, and carry on.

Calm down and carry on.

"No, I didn't read the papers. But I know what's *in* the papers."

"You know about that Mrs. Holt?"

"I know about that Mrs. Holt. Thorpe, someone gave me the wrong information."

"Someone gave *you* the wrong information! That's funny, that's *really* funny. Do you know the kind of trouble I'm in? I could be kicked right out of this school, Hagerman!"

"You are not in any trouble, Thorpe! You are an innocent party in a very nasty hoax!"

"Are *you* going to tell them I'm innocent?"

"*Them*, Thorpe? Who's them?"

"The police, Hagerman!"

"Sit down, Thorpe. Stop shouting and sit down. Do you want the whole house in on this?"

"The whole house is downstairs eating breakfast, Peter! I can't eat breakfast! I read the paper, and I puked!"

"Sit down, Thorpe."

Hagerman stretched out on his bed and put a damp washcloth over his face, leaving his mouth uncovered. He said, "Now listen to me. Carefully. There is a psycho loose in this city, and we were his victims. Now. This certain psycho, whom I have not laid eyes on, scrawled a note on the wall of the men's in a Socony station where I went for gas yesterday morning. Now. This note gave Matilda Holt's address, and this note said, 'The best piece of tail this side of the river. She works alone. Five dollars for fifteen minutes. She looks like anything but what she is. Tell her Turtle sent you.' . . . Thorpe, it happened that way, and I cannot express myself, but, Thorpe, I swear to you on a stack of Bibles, I had no idea that poor woman was the object of some obvious psycho's sick cruelty!"

"What about the phone calls? Did we make any phone calls to her?"

"Thorpe, may I ask you a question?"

"*What?*"

"Are you even remotely aware of my feelings about Vietnam? Do you know that I did a thirty-page paper on Peter Dawkins? Are you even *remotely* aware of how it turned my stomach to hear that burlesque of the song about the Green Berets, which you and Shepley were amusing yourself with the other afternoon?"

Thorpe sighed. "Yeah, I know."

"Do you honestly think I would willfully persecute the mother of one of our fighting men risking his life in Vietnam?"

"No. I guess not."

"You *guess* not, Thorpe? You *guess* not, mother-lover?"

"All right. I know you wouldn't. But what about those phone calls?"

"The person who made those phone calls, Thorpe, is obviously the sick, demented, cruel creature who defaced the wall of the Socony station men's room."

"What are we going to *do*, Peter?"

"We are not going to do anything, Daniel. We are certainly not going to bring disgrace on Pi Delta Pi, because we were the victims of a nasty hoax."

"Peter, she can identify me."

"She'll never see you again, Thorpe."

"How do I know? I could bump into her anyplace."

"Where? At the Unmuzzled Ox? At the Co-op? Out on our front lawn? In the Administration Building? Use your head, Thorpe. She is a sad little woman who hangs around Far Point with other sad little women; she shops in the A and P and Woolworth's and her whole world is that crummy main street which runs through Far Point, and how often do you traverse that crummy main street?"

"I go to the movies in Far Point."

"Then go to the drive-ins. They show better pictures, anyway."

"It's easy for you to be calm, Peter, but I—"

Peter Hagerman shot up into a sitting position. He said, "Have I got a wet rag over my face because I like wet rags over my face? Have I been swallowing Gelusil because it tastes good? Am I downstairs eating breakfast? Did I get any sleep last night after Bud told me about all of this? Are you OUT OF YOUR MIND, MOTHER-LOVER?"

"Okay, Peter. *Okay* . . . I didn't mean you weren't worried."

"I'm sick inside, Thorpe. I think of that poor woman, and it makes me *sick!*"

"Maybe we just ought to tell the police. They'd understand."

"They would, Thorpe? Are you SIMPLE?"

"Wouldn't they?"

"Thorpe, doesn't your dull brain entertain *any* notions of self-protection? Don't you realize that anyone in this fraternity could tell the police you're a Vietnik?"

"I don't agree with our policy in Vietnam; does that make me a Vietnik?"

"In the eyes of the police, it makes you a very logical

suspect, Daniel. And you were very drunk last night. You know you puked in the street? You know we were eighty-sixed from the Ox?"

"I hope to hell *you'd* stand up for me."

"You were back and forth to the men's a dozen times. How could I swear you didn't make a phone call, or ten phone calls? I wasn't taking you to the john and back, you know . . . Thorpe, the police wouldn't believe either one of us, and that's a fact! Daniel, for our own sake, and for the sake of Pi Delta Pi, we've got to keep this between you and me."

"Yeah, I suppose you're right."

"You *suppose*, Thorpe?"

"I know you're right."

"I hope to God you haven't already blabbed to Shepley!"

"I haven't told anyone."

"Good!" said Hagerman. "I just hope they catch that sick creep; I'd like to get *my* hands on him."

Things had a way of working in Hagerman's favor. After Thorpe left, while Hagerman was dressing, Burroughs came into the room, and shut the door, and sat down on his bed with a very long face.

Hagerman said, "What's the matter with you?"

"This is strictly confidential, Peter. All right?"

"All right."

"You remember our talk last night?"

"Sure."

"Well, you were sort of loaded, so I don't think you realized how upset I was. My old man really read me out. He's pretty good-natured, so when he busts a gut it shakes me up. You passed out and I didn't sleep at all, and I got to worrying about my Spanish grades, because I'm darn close to flunking, and that'd be all I'd need."

"So?"

"So it was late; it was after two, but I was wide awake and I figured I'd go over my vocabulary. I went up to study hall for about an hour. I was just putting the light out when I heard someone coming up the stairs. I wouldn't have thought anything, but it was the way he was coming up the stairs, like he was sneaking up the stairs."

"*Who* was sneaking up the stairs?"

"Shepley. Peter, he went into Blouter's suite, and he turned on the light, and he shut the door. He was in there for a while, a few minutes, and finally I opened the door, and he was fumbling around in Blouter's closet."

"What'd he say when he saw you?"

"He got very red in the face, and he said something about having a lot to drink, and being in the wrong room."

"Is *that* right?"

"But he wasn't drunk, Peter. He came up those stairs as quiet as a cat. I don't think he could have managed that drunk."

"He couldn't have, Bud. He couldn't have."

"I don't think he could, either."

"Bud, are you thinking the same thing I am?"

"What are you thinking?"

"That we caught our klep."

"I don't know that I'd go *that* far."

Hagerman said, "I'd go that far. Bud, I think we ought to call a chapter meeting."

"Let's wait for Blouter to get back. Let's ask Blouter. We can't do anything without Blouter anyway, and anyway, maybe he *was* drunk."

"So Shepley's the klep. Very interesting. I knew that mother wasn't any good the second I set eyes on him!"

"We can't jump to conclusions, Peter."

"I'm not going to jump; I'm there, Bud. I knew that mother was a sneaky mother!"

"But let's not jump the gun, okay? Okay, Peter? Let's watch him."

"I want to think about it," Hagerman said. "I want to give it lots of thought. I won't jump the gun, Bud."

But there were always stumbling blocks, weren't there? There was always something you could not predict; there was *always* something in the way, just when you thought the way was clear. It was the story of your whole rotten little life, from kindergarten to grade school to Choate to Sandstone Military Academy to Overland Military Academy to Frick School to Far Point College. You just never had any PEACE. You just never had a CHANCE to calm down and carry on. Every time you picked yourself up, you got another push; it was beautiful the way the mothers wouldn't let you rest; wasn't it?

"I've been outside waiting for Burroughs to leave, Hagerman, that's where I've been."

"No, Shepley. I didn't mean where were you this morning., I meant where were you last night?"

"I was home, Hagerman. I was visiting my family in New York."

"I meant where were you about three o'clock last night?"

"I was in Blouter's suite, Hagerman. Didn't Burroughs tell you?"

"He told me, mother. What were you doing in Blouter's suite. I'm very interested in your answer to that. So is Burroughs."

"I was looking for the letter my mother wrote to Blouter. You know, about the silverware?"

"You still think such a letter was written, hah? You're sick."

"My mother admitted it, Hagerman. I was all worked up when I got back to the house last night, so I went up to Blouter's suite to see if I could find the letter. You know how it is when you're all worked up? I didn't know what I was going to do with the letter. A letter like that is very embarrassing. You can appreciate that. Very humiliating. I guess I wanted to destroy that letter. But then Burroughs surprised me, and I gave him some cock-and-bull story about being drunk and being in the wrong room. It was a good thing I didn't blurt out the reason I was really there, wasn't it?"

Hagerman mumbled, "I have a class; I have a ten-thirty."

"I'm cutting my classes today, Hagerman."

"Mother, I don't CARE what you're doing!"

"You'd better care. I might have a nervous breakdown, Hagerman. A joke is a joke, see, but now that I know it's really true, I'm very tense."

"I paid you a hundred and fifty dollars! That ended the matter!"

"Not for me, not after my mother told me it was true. I might have a real breakdown, same as Osmond. Remember how Osmond carried on? You were responsible for his breakdown, too. You could get quite a reputation, Hagerman. With the kind of reputation you could get, I think Blouter would probably consider deactivating you. What do you think?"

Hagerman flung the book he was carrying to the floor.

"Temper, temper, Hagerman. I haven't lost *my* temper. I had *myself* under control. You really have to admire me, too, for controlling myself last night when I was so worked

up. I could have spilled my guts to Burroughs, but I didn't.
Burroughs probably thought I was robbing Mike. Isn't that
what Bud thought?"

Hagerman said, "You better leave me alone, Shepley.
You're carrying this thing too far."

"Is that what you told Osmond? You see, you can't reason
with someone who feels very tense. About the only thing
you can do with someone who's very tense is give them something to take away the tension. My tension would probably
go away for a few hundred dollars."

"I don't have that kind of money. You MOTHER! I don't
have any money left."

"I'm very, very tense, Hagerman. I really am."

Hagerman said, "Shep, listen, I'm not rich. If I were
rich—"

Shepley interrupted him. "Don't whine, Hagerman. It in-
creases my tension."

"I gave you my LAST CENT YESTERDAY!"

"We could drive into New York, Hagerman. I bet your
family would lend you some money. If my family's willing
to give silverware for me, yours ought to be willing to do
something to help you out. That's what families are for,
don't you think? If you can't count on your family, who can
you count on?"

"You're blackmailing me!"

"That's a very perspicacious observation, Hagerman."

"You're BLACKMAILING ME, YOU MOTHER!"

Shepley answered, "It's a little something I learned from
my mother, you mother."

Fifteen

Dearest Janice,

It's strange how you can hate someone, and then when you understand what makes him tick, you find your hatred for him dissolving into sympathy. Into pity.

Today I took it upon myself to confront a pledge, whom I had reason to believe was stealing from other members of the fraternity. Our president is away in St. Louis, and as Pledge Director, I felt it was my duty to cope with the situation. I frankly admit that I never liked this pledge very much. That is a matter of record. I have a way of detecting bad character, and from the start, I was uneasy in the presence of Charles Shepley.

Often I had the feeling—I can't explain why—that he was a very dangerous person. A violent person. Perhaps a psychopath, though that sounds rather dramatic. But I did have such a feeling about Charles Shepley.

I deplore violence, unless it is a necessary means to a worthwhile end, such as it is in Vietnam, for instance.

For this reason, I believe that I actually hated Charles Shepley. Can you imagine me hating someone? Probably not, but there you are; the human mind is filled with contradictions and complexities.

But I no longer hate Charles Shepley. I pity him perhaps more than I have ever pitied another person.

Yes, he is the one who has been stealing from us. He admitted this to me. It was almost as though he were waiting for someone to accuse him, so that he could let go the terrible mental burden he has been shouldering since his arrival at Pi Delta Pi. Have you ever seen a man cry? I hope you never do. It is not a pretty sight.

In a few hours, I am going to drive him into New York, where he lives. I have promised him that I would not tell anyone, until he is away from here. I have promised to send on his things, so that he need not experience any embarrassment, nor be forced into any explanations. There is yet another sad note to this story. The other night, his family revealed to him that his membership in this fraternity depended on their gift of a set of silverware. We have all known this, and of course, we kept it from him. I never approved of the arrangement, but the majority voted for it, even though Charles Shepley was not Pi Pi material.

It is my guess that upon making this discovery, or rather, upon being inflicted with this information by his family, he wanted to be caught stealing. My roommate found him in the president's suite, rifling the closet. He was red-faced, and offered the weak excuse that he had drunkenly found his way into the wrong room.

I am not sorry I confronted him. I think he might have had a serious breakdown. Nor am I sorry that I was taught a lesson by this experience: there is a reason for everything a man does. There are stumbling blocks in the way of men which we have no way of divining, pressures upon men which we have no way of appreciating, fears and anxieties in the hearts of men which we would never guess were there. Some men will never be able to calm down and carry on; others will struggle to survive, and learn to cope, and do what they must to exist.

I have more to say, but I will finish this when I get back.

I have to laugh at myself for once feeling that Charles Shepley was dangerous or violent. Usually, I am right, but not this time. Poor guy!

More later—

When Bud Burroughs returned from his three-thirty class,

he saw the letter under the note that Hagerman had left him, requesting that Burroughs conduct the Purgatorio.

It was a very simple Purgatorio; the pledges were to solicit funds on campus for medical supplies to aid the fighting men in Vietnam.

Sixteen

At three fifteen, Shepley and Hagerman set off for New York in Hagerman's car.

Hagerman drove very slowly. The vaunt, the puff, the bluster were gone from him; he was sniveling and obsequious. His face had taken on a pinched look, and as he sat behind the wheel of the Corvair, with his short little legs working the brake and the gas pedal, he seemed suddenly very tiny, which he was, which until now he had always managed to camouflage behind a facade of bravado.

Shepley felt sorry for him. It was only a feeling, and not a thought, for he was not thinking of anything at all anymore, but doing whatever came into his head, as he had since leaving his family last night. What he had discovered about the contrivings of everyone did, it was true, go through his mind, but now as indifferently and lifelessly as an item of foreign news read in a newspaper. He was equally indifferent to his own stratagems, except to see that he was successful at them; thinking about all of it came too hard and was so futile.

"I don't know how much I'll be able to get, Shepley."

"Do the best you can. Then we'll see."

"I don't know what my family's going to think."

"We'll soon see."

"They might not give me anything; what if they don't give me anything?"

"They'll give you something."

"They're different from what you think."

"They couldn't be. I haven't thought about them."

"I mean, they're not devoted to me. They've never liked me."

"They love you. Don't ask for the moon."

"Love me? Nobody's ever loved me but Janice."

"I don't want to hear about it."

"All right, I won't talk."

"I don't care if you talk. Just don't give me your life history."

"They might not even be home. I know my father won't be home."

"We'll soon see."

They went on like that, almost politely. Hagerman was chain-smoking, and Shepley rolled down the window rather than complain about the smell of the Gauloises. He leaned his head out and took a deep breath of the warm March air, and periodically he noticed the view of the river and the varying blues in the distance, intertwined with the stark gray arms of leafless trees and the green of pines and evergreens.

"Shepley?"

"What?"

"I have to make a stop."

"What kind of a stop?"

"I have to find a john."

"Pull over and go behind a bush; do we have to make a production out of it?"

Hagerman looked embarrassed. He said, "I can't. I have to find a john. There's one near here."

"All right. You have to make boom-boom, huh?"

"There's one right off this exit. There's an abandoned filling station about five minutes off this exit."

"My family used to call it making boom-boom. What was your family's word for it?"

"I don't remember."

Shepley laughed. "*You* remember. But it embarrasses you, doesn't it, Hagerman?"

Hagerman said, "No. Why should it?"

"What'd they call it?"

"I said I didn't remember."

"You're just another poor jackass, aren't you, Hagerman?"

"Aren't *you*, Shepley?"

"Yes. Yes, indeed."

Hagerman swung off at the exit.

"What do you mean it's abandoned?" Shepley said.

"It's abandoned, that's all."

"Well, now, there won't be any toilet paper, Hagerman."

"It's the nearest one."

"You really have to go bad, huh?"

"Does that give you pleasure, Shepley?"

"Hagerman, I liked it better when you called me mother. This new you is very colorless, Hagerman. Can't you do something about it?"

"I wish you'd lay off, Shepley. I don't feel well."

"I wish you'd lay off, Shepley, *please.*"

"I wish you'd lay off, Shepley, please."

"This is the living end, Hagerman; this really is!"

But it wasn't. Oddly enough, it was like everything that had happened in the last sixteen hours—it was flat. It was the way Lois had described her time at the Cheetah, while they were lying in bed last night at the Bluebird. "Dull fireworks!" she had said, and he had stifled an impulse to say, "So's this." Meaning the way she had done everything he liked and then some, and he had, too, and it was not because they were not high—they were drinking right along with it—but there was none of the old wild euphoria, just sort of a wisenheimer awareness of it all, of her female machinations and his male response, as though it were all happening inside a breeding case, and yet at the same time some larger him was on the outside, peering in, observing with detachment.

—I love you, Charles.

(You don't love anybody, Lois.)

—I love you, too, very much.

(Neither do I.)

—We've never said that before to one another. I'm glad we waited.

(I wish we hadn't said it.)

—I'm glad, too.

(Nowhere to go from here but down, now).

And Hagerman had lost his swagger; he looked like an ugly little kid whom nobody ever wanted to play with, scurrying off with the green-apple trots, already working his belt open before he got inside the door.

Shepley sat smoking a cigarette he did not really want, fiddling with the dial on the radio to find some music. The next song you hear will give you a message about the coming events of your life in the month of April. Listen!

> Hi, ho, hey, hey,
> Chew your little troubles away.
> Hi, ho, hey, hey,
> Chew Wrigley's Spearmint Gum!

Shepley thought of an afternoon at Holy Child when he had gone to visit Billy with his mother. Billy used to love gum. When they lived on Riverside Drive, at any hour of the day you could put your hand down under a tabletop or a chair, and there would be a wad of gum stuck there, lucky old wad of satiated Spearmint blessed by Billy's pearly fangs. Anyway, that afternoon at Holy Child, Charles's mother had kept on trying to put a stick of licorice gum in Billy's gaping mouth, and when she got no response, she said, "I'll chew it for you, darling, but I'll leave the taste in it for you; don't you worry," and she had chewed it and pulled it out, and put it on Billy's lips and tried to push it in, and it had fallen out all full of drool.

That was all.

Just a random memory.

It was taking Hagerman a long time. Shepley got out of the car and stretched his legs, leaned down and picked up some gravel, and tossed the pieces one by one at a telephone pole.

It was a seedy filling station; the idle gas pumps were peeling and the rubber hoses were rotted; there was a dead bird near the door with maggots and flies all over it, and there were tall weeds which had pushed their way through the tar and formed little clusters where cars used to drive in and wait for service.

Shepley looked at his watch. Hagerman had been in there for ten minutes. Shepley decided to goose him, and he walked across to the small square brick building and went inside. The door marked MEN was shut, and Shepley stood just outside of it and called Hagerman's name.

There was no answer. Shepley waited another few seconds.

Then he shouted, "What the hell are you doing in there, Hagerman?" and still Hagerman did not answer.

Shepley tried the door; it was locked.

"Hagerman, what the hell are you doing?"

There was no sound.

Shepley rattled the doorknob and banged his fist against the door.

"Hagerman? . . . Hagerman, are you in there?"

And he thought of the pinched look on Hagerman's face,

and Hagerman whining, "I wish you'd lay off Shepley. I don't feel well," and he began to alternately kick at the door and shove it with his shoulders. It started to give, and Shepley applied more force, until the lock broke.

The putrid stench of stale excreta hit his nostrils full force at the same time something heavy and hard and merciless hit his head.

You were a gambler was what you were; you had always been one. You could suffer a surfeit of the worst sort of trepidations, and it would always make sense why you did when you won, for there was a thrill that went all through you, that lifted you right off the ground, like in dreams when you flew and it was easy and sweet and you were invulnerable. You forgot it at times; at times you thought you were a loser and your luck had been spent, but that was part of it, was what made times like this the exalted moments that were your reason for existence. Anything less was some weak stave you'd fall from leaning on, but you could lean on the power which charged you when you pulled off yet another *coup*, and weren't you cool!

Hagerman got down off the chair. He did not put the monkey wrench back inside his overcoat, but left it lying there beside Shepley. Blood trickled from the back of Shepley's head. He might well be dead, though Hagerman doubted that, and did not care, either way.

Hagerman walked across and kicked over a white pail once used for discarded paper towels. He turned a rickety chair on its side. He stood before the dirty mirror hanging on the wall, reached under his coat and ripped his shirt and tore his tie. Then he took out a small pocketknife and snapped the blade to, and slit some threads near the shoulder of his coat, and pulled until the material gave. Momentarily, he studied his face; then hating to do it, he nicked it with his knife, then took his fingernail and scratched the nick open; he did the same thing to his forehead. He wrenched a leather button from his coat, and tossed it on the floor.

He stood and looked at everything, and then he left the place, and drove his car a mile down the road, pulled over, cut the motor, and shook up a cigarette from the package in his pocket.

Then the old faithful computer took all the data in and gave it back, gift-wrapped.

—Oh, God! My old trouble! I have to get to a john fast.

—Sure, Peter. Is there some place near?

—There's an old abandoned gas station off the next exit. I'm sorry, Charles. I know you're upset.

—I feel better; in fact, I feel as though a weight's been lifted from my shoulders.

—I'm glad. I'm glad I could help. You were bound to get caught eventually.

—I know it.

—Here we are. I'll try not to be long.

—Take your time.

Hagerman went inside the filling station; he had been to this place once before, so he knew it was open; he knew it was filthy and he was prepared for the foul odor, but he had this condition, this thing he had never told anyone about but Bud Burroughs, and urgency could not afford to shop around for quality.

The thought occurred to him that he had left Shepley in the car, with the keys. For a moment, he almost went back for the keys, but then he rebuked himself for such an idea; Shepley was so obviously beaten and tractable.

Hagerman locked the door of the men's after himself, out of habit more than anything else. He relieved himself, and he was just on the verge of reaching for his overcoat, which he had hung on a hook in the small stall he had used, when he heard Shepley's voice.

—Hagerman?

—Just a minute, Charles.

—Hagerman?

—Just a minute, Charles.

He put his coat on; he was starting toward the door when he heard Charles shout:

—You picked a nice spot, Hagerman. Start saying your prayers, Hagerman.

And damn it all, Hagerman did not feel very brave; he, damn it all, actually began to tremble.

Then Shepley tried the door.

—Open the door, Hagerman.

—Please, Charles.

Yes, he had said please; he was that scared.

But Shepley kicked in the door, and came at him carrying a monkey wrench.

The only thing that saved Hagerman was the fact Shepley kept talking, kept reading Hagerman out, saying he was going to kill Hagerman, but first Hagerman was going to really appreciate how much Shepley hated him. He kept bouncing Hagerman against the wall, knocking things over, grabbing his clothes and pulling him in and pushing him back, with his eyes like the eyes of someone who had gone soft in the head.

He was ape; he had really flipped.

All right, Hagerman cried—admit it. And Hagerman begged —admit it. And yeah, Hagerman did say his prayers. And God isn't dead, because suddenly Charles Shepley slipped and fell to his knees, and the monkey wrench landed at Hagerman's feet, and Hagerman picked it up.

You're a little man, but when you're fighting for your goddam life, well, mother, you hit like a man twice your size.

Okay?

Okay, but wait a minute. Let's savor it a minute . . . You are a mother, mother; Peter, mother, you leave your mark, you *do* . . . and no Len Lovely, it *don't* rub out.

Then Hagerman turned the key in the ignition, and headed into Far Point to meet the father of his roommate.

Seventeen

He woke up in a field, at the bottom of a hill, not far from the filling station. He remembered staggering there, remembered the warm feeling of his own blood trickling down his neck and soaking into his shirt collar through his jacket, and the pain throbbing at the back of his head. His only thought then had been to get away, out of sight of the road, in case Hagerman came back to finish what he had started. He had seen a housing development down past the hill, and he had headed for it. But he had collapsed, exhausted and quite faint from the realization that he had nearly been murdered, that maybe he would, after all, die, that his blood was leaking out of him.

Now he was stronger. The back of his head was sticky, but dry; the blood had clotted. He stood and the vertigo he had felt earlier had vanished; the pain was mild. He removed his jacket and saw that there was not a lot of blood on it. He put it back on, and he walked easily, though the memory of his terror upon awakening on the floor in the filling station lingered.

What he wanted to do was get out of Far Point, go somewhere, anywhere, but not home. He had five dollars and some change; the rest of his money was at Pi Delta Pi. That all seemed very far away; his mind did not want the task of sorting all that out, of thinking about the right thing to do, the practical thing to do, or of trying to imagine what Hagerman was doing.

Lois. He wanted to be with her. He trudged through the field toward the lights ahead, trying to fathom the reason for a sketchy feeling of indifference he had had earlier when he remembered last night and being with her. He had turned it into something very different than the way it had been; he was sure of that. It had been very good between them, better than it had ever been. Yet he did remember, even now, thinking that it was the beginning of the end with them, that she had announced her love, and whatever he stole from that point on he would be stealing for himself. And he had gone directly from the Bluebird to Blouter's suite, as he had planned to do before the Bluebird, but something was different about it. She was missing from the adventure; it was not for her. It was not even for anything he wanted; it just was, the way it just was when he made the demand on Hagerman after breakfast.

He remembered a moment with Hagerman when he was fooling around about having a nervous breakdown, and his own voice had sounded like a stranger's voice saying something wholly believable.

And he remembered, too, a feeling he had had when he was standing outside the men's in the filling station, and the thought had occurred that Hagerman might really be very ill in there, and occurring with this thought was one of giving up the whole venture, of letting poor Hagerman off the hook, really of getting off it himself, before he couldn't.

These remembrances had a soothing effect, for he had not been all the way in; there had been some part of him protesting, the part of him that had led him yesterday afternoon to his father's lab, the part that was carrying him across this field right now, because he felt that he was going to be all right; he was going to get himself back somehow— somewhere along the way he had lost himself, and nearly lost his life in the bargain.

He saw a Mr. Frostee stand to the left of the housing development; he saw an outdoor phone booth next to it, and he headed that way. It was six-thirty.

It was seven before he was able to reach her, after eight by the time she arrived to pick him up. He had washed in Mr. Frostee.

"I'm not a taxi, you know!"

"I know."

He shut the door.

"No, you don't know, or you would have called a taxi!"

"Are we going to sit here and argue?"

"My God, Charles! *My God,* what *happened* to you?"

"A lot. Let's go someplace where we can talk."

"Let's go to a hospital! What *happened* to you?"

"Let's just *go* someplace, Lois. Not a hospital."

"That's blood on your shirt!"

"Yes, but I'm all right. I'll button my coat; I'm all right."

"No, you're *not!*"

"I am. I am. I'm not the martyr type."

"What type are you?"

He said, "I'll get to that."

He began to get to it once they got to the park.

He poured himself a drink and lit a cigarette; on the way there he had told her that he had had a fight with Hagerman, but he had not gone into all the details, because he wanted to start way back.

She said, "Are you sure your head doesn't hurt?"

"Yes. I'm okay. Okay?"

"Are you surprised that I wore my mink?"

"Not too."

"You don't want me to tell you why I wore it, do you? Because we're talking seriously."

"Why did you wear it?"

"You really don't want to know. I can tell by your voice."

"I really want to know."

He found himself smiling, despite the growing suspicion that all that he planned to say to her was not going to amount to a hill of beans, because you didn't reach a Lois Faye ever, which was probably the reason he was attracted to her in the first place. He had had no destination in mind when he had met her. Now? He didn't know what he wanted from her at this point, only that he wanted to be with her, which entailed listening to the reason she had worn her mink.

She said, "I wore it because I've never worn it when I was in love. And I wasn't in a good mood either, having to go all the way out to some Mr. Frostee stand!"

"I want to tell you something before we start talking about love, Lois."

"You're married, aren't you?"

"Can we be serious?"

"I'm sorry about your head. Why wouldn't you let me take you to a hospital?"

"My head's all right."

"We could have stopped on the way, and gotten me some Southern Comfort."

"I'm sorry. I didn't even notice you weren't drinking. Have some of mine."

"This car isn't much of a bar; one empty bottle, one bottle half-full."

"Have some of mine."

"I hate it without water! I hate it anyway, but I hate it without water worse!"

"We should carry a thermos for emergencies. Do you want to drive in and get some Southern Comfort?"

"Charles! We have a thermos! It had ice cubes in it, and I put it in the back with the picnic hamper."

"And the picnic hamper has cheese in it, and I'm half-starved!"

"I'm glad I wore my mink," she said, as Charles got out of the car to get the things from the trunk.

They drank from paper cups. Charles diluted his whiskey, too, because he was drinking on an empty stomach; he quartered the cheese and passed her some, and then he began again, he began with Billy and he got up to the part where the move to Eighty-second Street from Riverside Drive became necessary because of the drain on his grandfather's estate.

"Is your drink sweet?" she interrupted him.

"I didn't notice."

"I think there was sugar in that water."

"Can I finish?"

"So far, it's a *very* depressing story. So far, I don't see what it has to do with you and me."

"It has a lot to do with you and me. I think."

"I don't think it does."

"You want to get down to brass tacks?"

"What is the sum and substance? Let's talk turkey, Charles. Let's get down to cases, and go over the cardinal points."

He sighed, "This isn't funny . . . . I'm leaving Far Point, Lois."

As he said that, he felt a salty taste in his mouth, and a pressure in his head.

"No, you're *not!*" she said.

"I can't stay here." And something was happening to the

light; there was a queer prismatic look to the park lamp down the road. He probably should have gone to the hospital.

She said, "Yes, you can; what do you mean you *can't?*"

The air seemed to crackle. He managed to say, "I'm a thief."

"What?"

"Yes, I am. Turn off the radio, will you?"

"The radio isn't on. Are you *crazy?*"

"I've been stealing so I could take you out. I don't have any money. I've been stealing everywhere. Everywhere."

His words seemed to come out very, very slowly, but he was telling her all about it, and it took a long, long time, but he was telling her everything, until he could no longer hear his own voice over her laughter. She kept laughing and laughing and laughing at him, laughing and laughing, and laughing, and laughing.

Charles began to sob. Everything before his eyes turned into bright jelly, and his mother's face appeared then on the radio dial, or was Lois there, her head on a great pendulum, larger than the car, hovering over the car, laughing at him?

Charles said, "I can't pay you to love me."

The pendulum was actually one of her breasts, with her face on it; the nipple, her nose. He saw himself on her breast, crawling across it like a baby, crawling up into her nose.

"Lois," he said, "let me out. I feel awful."

She said, "I'm a big phony!"

"Why are you laughing at me?"

"I'm taking off everything. I don't want to wear these clothes."

"You better stop laughing. I know what you think of me. You traded me for silverware."

"Everything comes off. I'm going to be naked!"

"Stop laughing!"

But she could not stop, and she *was* going to be naked. And it took a long, long time to get out of her clothes, and all the while Charles was glaring at her. He was a rabbi, and if there was anything she could not stand it was a rabbi stoking a fire, but that was what she deserved, to be incinerated like all the Jews.

She said, "I'm afraid."

Charles's voice said, "You hate me."

"I don't, Charles. Where are you?"

"Don't come near me."

"Charles, I need to hang on to you. I'm out of whack, way out of whack!"

"Don't get near me, I said! I'm tired of being used. One wants a mother's pin, and one wants a Pucci, and no one wants me."

"I want you, Charles. I know I'm boring. I am. I make jokes to try and cover it up. I don't want the right things. I'm a phony. If you don't love me, I'm going into the fire with all the Jews. I'm a dirty kike! We're all alike. We want money. Charles, let me hang on to you. I love you."

"Don't!"

"Charles, please!"

"You want to decapitate me! I need my head! I need it to think with!"

"Charles, the knife is so pretty. Look at the colors. There's cheese left on it, and now there's a trillion little jewels right there where the cheese was."

"You're a spider."

"I'm lonely, Charles. I'm not worthwhile. for I have no real values and I am empty as a shell. I know I am. I've been told that I am, and I am. Hold me so I'm full, Charles."

"You see this knife? In my fantasies I held a knife like this to kill Billy with. Don't you hurt my head. Don't you put your hands near me. I can't kill Billy, but I have this knife for protection."

"I want to put my arms around you. I never told my father I loved him because he made me a Jew. I'm not a nice person at all, not at all. I see snakes hanging from the trees, Charles. I see snakes, Charles! I think I'm out of whack! I see myself dead on the fender! Am I dead?"

"Let go of me!"

"I'm afraid!"

"Let—go—of me!"

"Charles!"

"I *told* you! I *need* my head!"

Then he said, "My head is there, but I'm out of my mind."

It took a long, long time to pull out the knife.

She was naked, and she would soon be very cold, so he forced enough energy out of himself to put her coat on her.

Mink. Because she was with someone she loved.

Eighteen

"Maybe it's my height," said Peter Hagerman.

Ida Burroughs said, "Maybe what's your height?"

"Maybe that's why no one pays any attention to what I say."

Arnold Burroughs said, "We take full responsibility for this. I don't care if a dwarf walks in and says he thinks he just killed Fatty Arbuckle, it's up to us to investigate."

Bud Burroughs said, "I'd investigate that myself, since Fatty Arbuckle's been dead about ten years."

Arnold Burroughs shot his son a disapproving look; there was nothing funny in the situation.

Ida Burroughs saw her husband's expression, and she said, "Buddy doesn't mean to joke about something so serious. It's just that it's Easter, and we ought to *try* and smile."

That was a terrible thing for Arnold to say, about the dwarf. That poor little boy didn't come to Buddy's shoulder. He was a nice boy, too, not at all the way Ida Burroughs had pictured him. He had the manners of a prince.

Arnold Burroughs said, "If I'd been on duty, I'd have done more than drive out to that filling station and look around."

"They could see the blood," said Hagerman. "Excuse me, Mrs. Burroughs. I know this is a very distasteful conversation."

"You should know the things we discuss at this table, Peter.

154

I've developed a very strong stomach. . . . Why don't you have another slice of ham?"

"Thank you, but I've had too much already."

Arnold Burroughs said, "Oh, I know what they thought. They thought you boys had gotten into a little tussle, and it'd all come out in the wash. The kid was gone and all. They probably figured it wasn't worth following up."

"If they'd only let me see you, sir. You would have followed it up."

"Darn right!"

Ida Burroughs said, "That girl would be alive today if they'd called Arnold. That maniac never would have gotten to her if they hadn't been so afraid to wake up Arnold. I don't know what it is about a policeman sleeping in the daytime. They respect that. But they don't think anything of calling up at two, three in the morning, when Arnold works a day shift. . . . That poor girl."

Bud Burroughs said. "What did she go into the park with him for in the first place? He couldn't have acted very normal."

Hagerman said, "Nuts are very tricky."

"They are for a fact," said Arnold Burroughs. "I wouldn't be surprised if he was the same one who went after Matilda Holt. It'll probably turn out that he was."

"I was thinking that, too, sir," said Hagerman.

Arnold Burroughs liked being called "sir"; he wouldn't mind at all if a little of Hagerman's character rubbed off on Bud. He could even bear the stinky cigarettes; Hagerman was a New Yorker, and he had a little polish; you couldn't hang a man for that.

"I still can't figure out how he got my gold lighter," said Hagerman. "I always carried it with me. I never left it in my room."

"How'd he get all that loot?" Burroughs said. "Jesus, he had everything but Mother Varner's teeth stashed away in that drawer of his."

"Don't say Jesus on Easter Sunday, dear," said Ida Burroughs.

"Remember Thorpe's face?" Hagerman laughed. He turned to Arnold Burroughs and said, "After I came back from the police station, I told Thorpe that I wanted to go through Shepley's things. I said I didn't think we'd find anything—I thought Shepley was too clever for that; well, sir, Thorpe said we wouldn't find anything, because he'd have known

if he was living with a klep, and then I opened the top drawer, and my God! Excuse me, Mrs. Burroughs."

"I don't mind 'my God.' It's 'Jesus' I don't like."

Bud Burroughs said, "Thorpe's eyes were as big as saucers!
Out came Peter's lighter, and then a cigarette case, and then
a few wallets, and like I said, everything but Mother Varner's
teeth."

"Stealing from his own fraternity brothers," said Ida Burroughs.

"Ida, the boy isn't all there. You know? Screw loose?"

Hagerman said, "Sir, I'd be curious to know what he said
when you found him in the park. Did he mention me?"

"Naw. Nope. He was too far gone. He didn't talk gib-
berish or anything. He knew he'd murdered the girl. He
kept saying that it wasn't her fault. He kept saying that he'd
gone crazy, that he *was* crazy, and that he needed help.
He was in a state of shock."

"Well," said Ida Burroughs, "Far Point's had its share of
excitement these last few days. I thought that poor Mrs.
Holt was bad enough, but then all of this happened, and I
guess we just never have had anything like this happen, ever.
Have we, Arnold?"

"Not that I can remember."

"Blouter sure picked a good weekend to go see mommy
and daddy," said Hagerman.

"What do your folks do for Easter, Peter?" Ida Burroughs
asked.

"They go out."

"Maybe I shouldn't have asked."

"I don't mind. I've never had much of a home life. I was
always shipped off to school."

"If you were my son, I wouldn't have let you out of my
sight. I think you're a darling boy."

"Well, thank you, Mrs. Burroughs. I suppose I shouldn't
admit it, but this is the very nicest Easter I've ever spent."

"Why *shouldn't* you admit it, Peter. It makes me very
happy."

"It looks like a bid for sympathy or something."

Arnold Burroughs said, "You consider this your home
away from home, Peter. We like having you here."

Hagerman was close to tears.

Really.

You go along thinking there's something wrong with you,
because nobody's ever taken much trouble with you, and

then one day you wake up and you discover you were doing
the only thing you could do, because instinctively you knew
you had to protect yourself; *instinctively* you knew that.
What other way was there to explain this whole thing?

You were up against something you didn't even *know* the
size of; you were running against a mother the likes of
which you couldn't have even imagined: a mother who would
hack up a defenseless girl! A klep mother; a clever, dia-
bolical goddam klep-mother-murderer! And a little peanut
like you had held your own, with nobody to help you, with
nobody there for you, with no place to go on Easter Sunday
but to your roommate's home.

For all Len Lovely cared, for all Peg Beauty cared, you
were an ant; hell, you were a cockroach. You were that
mother in the mud in Vietnam; the mud-Turtle, with some
bespectacled creep back home by her radio borrowing glory
from your battles. Oh, I *love* Joey . . . just as long as Joey
doesn't come home and sit in any of the goddam chairs and
soil the antimacassars!

Beautiful! Wasn't it?

Well, Joeys, peanuts, ants, cockroaches, they come
through, and they always will, and they'll do it on their
own goddam power too; they'll take crumbs; sure, they'll
probably even choke up when somebody else's mother says
they're darling boys. You going to blame them?

But you listen here, mothers. There are some of us, not
many of us, just a few of us, who'll smell you mothers out;
we'll get better and better and better at smelling you out,
and the kind of chance a Shepley got once a Shepley won't
get a second time, because that old monkey wrench will
kill him dead. Because you learn, don't you? The mothers
are a lot bigger and a lot more dangerous than you ever
dreamed, and they're never going to get a chance at you
again.

Nobody helps you; you might get a few crumbs tossed your
way, but you bake your own cake. Solo. Number two has
to try harder, right, Len Lovely?

Oh dear; oh dear, thought Ida Burroughs, now those are
tears in that boy's eyes.

She said, "Chocolate cake coming up! I hope you like
chocolate cake, Peter!"

"I like it very much, thank you, Mrs. Burroughs."

Bud Burroughs said, "Dad, what'll happen to Shepley?"

"What can they do with a kid like that? Lock him up the rest of his life, is all. We'll pay the taxes, and he'll get chicken à la king every Sunday."

Peter Hagerman said, "Somebody will always pay his way. He always had his way paid for him, and now it won't be any different. Beautiful!"

Bud Burroughs said, "He'll be out in a few years. His family's got money."

"I don't like that kind of talk, Bud, and I don't mind telling you that in front of Peter!" said Arnold Burroughs. "The law isn't perfect, but at least we try. I'm not proud of how we handled this thing, but we can't win them all, particularly when we're up against nuts. I've known nuts that could pass for you or me or your mother or Peter."

"Okay, I'm sorry. *Mea culpa.*"

"It's all cut and dried with chemistry, Bud," said Arnold Burroughs. "You can predict what's going to happen every step of the way. But who knows what a nut's going to do next?"

"Who knows?" said Peter Hagerman.